THE SWAP

*Explicit Stories from
the World of Swinging*

A Mischief Collection of Erotica

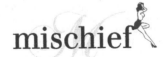

mischief

Mischief
An imprint of HarperCollins*Publishers*
77–85 Fulham Palace Road,
Hammersmith, London W6 8JB

www.mischiefbooks.com

A Paperback Original 2013

First published in Great Britain in ebook format by
HarperCollins*Publishers* 2012

A catalogue record for this book is
available from the British Library

ISBN-13: 9780007534852

Set in Sabon by FMG using Atomik ePublisher from Easypress

CONTENTS

Playdar
Lisette Ashton

These two aren't players. You're wasting your time with them.

Sophie read Rob's text message, struggling not to reveal any telltale sign in her facial expression. The effort of maintaining a poker face, she knew, made her features appear haughty and long. It was not an attractive look and she tried to lose it as quickly as possible. But the expression was clearly there long enough for Philip and Angela to notice.

'Is there a problem?'

She glanced up from her mobile towards Philip as he raised the concerned question. He had a shaved head and a smile that suggested mischief and danger. His muscular physique was squeezed into a pale casual suit.

His whole image was the stylish and exciting persona of a relaxed Englishman abroad.

Beside him, his Barbie-blonde wife, Angela, tilted her head. 'Is everything OK?' she asked. 'You were frowning.'

'Everything's fine,' Sophie assured them both. 'I was just trying to think of the right way to respond to this idiot I'm dealing with.' She waggled the phone to indicate the idiot she was referring to, and then comforted them with a reassuring grin before typing and sending her text message response.

These two swing like a shithouse door in a thunderstorm. I'll put money on it.

'You must be quite the businesswoman back in the UK,' Angela observed.

Sophie shrugged. 'I do all right. What about you two?'

Her phone gave two beeps. An incoming text message. She held up an apologetic finger to silence Philip and Angela while she read Rob's response.

£500 says you don't get to screw Philip before the end of the day. These two don't swing. They're too straitlaced.

As usual, it was a perfectly punctuated text from her husband. It included apostrophes of omission and a postgraduate vocabulary. Sophie felt confident the word 'straitlaced' was not included in the predictive text package on his Nokia. She thought most men who weren't Rob would try to put a hyphen in the word. His correctness with language was an essential part of his character.

She typed her reply with the practised ease of a veteran texter.

Call it £1K if I can get you with Angela. I say these two swing.

Rob's response came back in seconds.

It's a bet.

'I'm sorry,' Philip said. 'We're distracting you from your business.' He made as though he was about to get up and leave.

Sophie put out a reassuring hand. 'No. Please. That's the last text I'm sending this evening. I'm all yours now.' She was delighted to see Angela flush on hearing the comment. Sophie flashed her most disarming smile for the couple, as though the statement had been made in all innocence.

Her playdar, she knew, was 99.9% accurate. Maybe higher. It had never failed her so far and taking the money on this bet with Rob was almost guaranteed. Angela and Philip, she felt certain, both lived the lifestyle. They were both players.

'Rob should be back with our drinks in a moment and I promise you I won't be talking business for the rest of the night.' She met Philip's eye and said, 'If I go back on my word, you can take me over your knee and spank my bare backside as punishment.'

Angela stiffened.

Sophie could see the woman's hand fall to Philip's thigh and squeeze. Philip's smile widened. Angela's nails were painted a wanton scarlet. Her hand was so close to Philip's groin that Sophie could almost feel his excitement.

'With that sort of assurance,' Philip told Sophie, 'I'd be a fool to leave.'

Rob returned with a tray of drinks. He didn't bother making eye contact with Sophie. The bet was on and there was no point in either of them labouring the point or running the risk of spoiling the evening's fun. And, it was clear to Sophie, Rob was desperate to have Angela.

He complimented Philip's wife on her necklace: a series of princess-cut diamonds on white gold. His fingers lingered dangerously close to her cleavage as he boldly examined the piece. He leaned closer and Sophie saw his fingertips brush against the blonde's décolletage. She could imagine the heat of his breath was warming the blush of Angela's cleavage.

Sophie smiled.

She had always enjoyed watching Rob interact with other women. There was something satisfying about the way he was able to tease, please and excite them. It was particularly thrilling for her to know that he had the ability to excite and arouse so many women. And yet he always chose to return to her at the end of an evening.

4

It reminded her that the openness of their relationship was something special and not to be taken for granted.

Used to watching such casual adult play, and barely listening as Angela told Rob the necklace was a gift from Philip to commemorate their fifth wedding anniversary, she saw the woman's nipples stiffening. Angela was wearing a thin cotton dress. In the balmy heat of this African summer evening it was probably the most sensible fabric to wear, Sophie thought practically. Even though it was now early evening, and the sun's most ferocious hours had long since passed, the humidity remained cloying and interminable.

The white cotton fitted tight against Angela's chest. It was so tight Sophie had already noticed the woman wasn't wearing a bra. And, as Rob continued to examine the diamond necklace, Sophie could see that Angela's nipples were growing hard and swelling against the fabric. Her chest had been rising and falling regularly before. Now it looked like each inward breath was laboured by swelling passion. The pulse beneath Angela's ear seemed to throb with heightened expectation.

'You'll have to forgive my husband,' Sophie told Philip. 'He works as a jeweller and he never seems to take a break from his occupation.'

'I've got nothing against a man admiring my wife's jewels,' Philip admitted.

He gave Sophie his easy smile. It was a smile that she

longed to kiss. She could picture Philip wearing that smile, and nothing else, while he lay back on a bed and allowed her to suck on his length. The idea made the crotch of her panties warm and damp.

She wondered if, when Philip said he had nothing against a man admiring his wife's jewels, he was talking about the diamonds. Or if he had used the word 'jewels' as a euphemism for her breasts.

Had Philip just admitted that he and Angela were players?

She tried to think how she could surreptitiously raise the question so that Philip or Angela would answer honestly.

'I do like well-made jewellery,' Rob admitted. He spoke in a low voice, as though he was sharing a secret with Angela. 'I was thinking of giving Sophie a pearl necklace this morning. But that's got nothing to do with our talk about jewellery, has it?'

Angela choked back a lewd chuckle.

Philip's indulgent smile broadened, although Sophie suspected he hadn't heard the comment. And, while Philip's attention was distracted, Sophie knew Rob's finger would be dropping to 'accidentally' graze against Angela's stiff nipple.

It was a move he often made: surprisingly subtle but devastatingly effective.

Sophie was holding Philip's gaze when it happened

but she knew the moment when the contact occurred because she saw Angela stiffen. Her ears, attuned to the moment and waiting for the sound, heard Angela catch her breath. The sigh was rich with excitement and it sounded as though Angela was desperate to experience more.

'I'd love to see this outside in the sunlight,' Rob told Angela. 'Would you indulge me?' He glanced at Philip and asked, 'Would you mind if I took your wife? Outside I mean.'

Angela looked momentarily flustered. She gave her husband an apologetic smile and then turned to Sophie. 'You two don't mind, do you?'

Philip and Sophie were shaking their heads.

Angela placed a hand over her breast. Sophie couldn't work out if the woman was pointing to her necklace, or covering up the embarrassment of her pert, stiff nipples. She supposed the gesture could have been a combination of the two.

'I love these,' Angela said, gesturing at the diamonds. 'And it's so nice to show them off to someone who obviously appreciates them.'

'I'm sure Rob appreciates them,' Sophie said drily.

Philip nodded indulgently. He didn't seem perturbed when Rob gallantly took Angela by the elbow and escorted her out to the balcony. If anything, and Sophie felt sure the message was coming again from her playdar, it seemed that he was relieved that they were finally alone.

'Your husband has a good eye.'

'His other parts are OK, too,' Sophie quipped.

'Why are you out here?' he asked. 'Is it a holiday?'

'We needed to recharge our batteries. Rob and I both work hard and play hard.' She took a deep breath and said, 'We'd been putting in extra hours at the office and we'd been playing extra hard at the club.'

Philip nodded as though he knew what she meant.

Sophie allowed the words to linger between them, silently hoping that Philip would ask her about *playing extra hard at the club*. If he asked what she meant, she could tell him it was a swingers' club. She would explain that she and Rob spent their weekends there, usually sweltering in the heat of a group room, often sweating and writhing with a horde of eager, attractive strangers, all horny and each one desperate to fuck.

In her mind's eye she could picture the group room at her favourite club. It was always illuminated by red bulbs and looked as bloody and as dangerous as a horror movie. She couldn't count the number of times she had become lost in there, pressed between naked strangers, submitting to their inquisitive caresses and giving herself over to the pleasure they wanted to bestow. Every time she allowed her imagination to transport her there for a moment, the experience was sufficiently intense to leave her aroused and desperately craving satisfaction.

Philip didn't ask the question.

He didn't ask about her *playing extra hard at the club* and he didn't ask about her work. Instead, he seemed content to sit back in his seat, smiling easily for her, and relaxing with his drink.

'What is it you do when you're not holidaying in Africa?' she asked.

'I work in a prison.'

'You're a screw?'

She couldn't stop the cheeky grin from spreading across her lips. If there was one thing she enjoyed with the light-hearted banter of a potential new conquest it was the opportunity for double entendre. She loved to play with words and make the mundane sound lewd and suggestive. Using the word *screw* in a variety of suggestive ways promised to give her the chance to properly flirt with Philip.

'Are you a good screw?' she asked quickly. 'Or are you a hard screw? If you work shifts does that mean you can be an early-morning screw or a late-night screw? If you get a lot of pleasure from your work does that mean you're a passionate, satisfying screw ...?'

'Actually,' he began apologetically, 'I work in the prison's admin.'

She scowled. This wasn't going as she had hoped.

Over Philip's shoulder, Sophie saw Rob and Angela on the balcony outside. The African sunlight turned Angela's blonde hair white. Rob had made his trademark move, brushing Angela's hair over her ear, allowing his fingertips to trail against her cheek, then caress the sensitive flesh of her neck.

And then he was leaning in for the kiss.

Angela melted against him.

Sophie could sympathise with the woman. When Rob was turning on the charm it was impossible to resist him. Even watching the exchange, Sophie felt an echo of the thrill that Angela was clearly enjoying.

Rob's hand fell to Angela's breast. He caressed her through the fabric of her thin cotton top. Angela made no objection to his hand being there. Instead she leaned into him. One hand dropped below the level of the window and Sophie guessed that Angela was exploring the shape of Rob's erection.

She envied her husband taking advantage of Angela and the isolation of the hotel's balcony. She only wished Philip was as responsive.

'Have you and Angela been together long?' Sophie asked.

It crossed her mind that perhaps her playdar had misled her.

Certainly Angela was enjoying herself with Rob. Sophie figured, if she closed her eyes and listened intently, she would have heard Angela's stifled cries as she muffled her sighs of pleasure beneath Rob's touch.

But what Rob had with Angela was very different from what Sophie found she had with Philip.

Conversation with Philip was like pulling teeth.

She supposed it could be that he and Angela lived the lifestyle, but that Philip didn't find her attractive and had no interest in trying to have her. Sophie tried to quickly dismiss that thought, sure it was impossible for any man to resist her innate desirability. But it was enough to wound her self-confidence.

She glanced over Philip's shoulder and saw that Rob and Angela were still taking advantage of the balcony's solitude. Their passionate kiss had turned into a ferociously intimate interlude. The top of Angela's dress was pulled down exposing a bare, pert breast. Rob clutched at her with one hand, his fingers buried punishingly hard into her soft flesh. Sophie could tell, from the way he was bucking and thrusting against her, that her husband's erection was buried deep inside Angela.

A quickie.

A knee-trembler up against the wall of the hotel balcony.

Angela threw back her head. She released a sigh of obvious satisfaction. In the same moment Rob held himself rigid. Spasms seemed to ripple through his body. Sophie caught a glimpse of her husband's face and saw he was grinning tightly through a bitter and powerful elation. The expression made her want to kiss him and enjoy the aftermath of his pleasure.

'We've been together now for seven years.' Philip answered her question, diverting her attention away from the scene on the balcony and back to him. 'If I believed in the legend I suppose I'd be ready to have an affair by now.'

'Really?' Sophie guessed it was time to make a provocative move. 'I expect there's a waiting list of candidates desperate to fill that role for you. Where would I have to sign up?'

'Perhaps I could give you a probing interview later this evening?'

She grinned at him. She had been right. Her worries that her playdar had missed the mark were completely unfounded. Philip was assailing her with the James Bond-esque banter she always associated with making new friends from the lifestyle.

'It sounds like it could be quite a rigorous selection process.'

'It would be quite a demanding position.'

'But I suspect it would be a satisfying role.'

They were chuckling together at the jokes when Rob and Angela returned. If Philip noticed that his wife's hair was awry, or that the lipstick had been kissed from her lips, he was too gentlemanly to mention it. Sophie took the opportunity to brush invisible flecks of dust from the lapels of Rob's jacket, trying not to make the action look proprietorial. Rob was perspiring heavily, probably because of the cloying heat and the exertion of satisfying Angela, Sophie thought. And she wanted to kiss him and ask him how Angela had felt wrapped around his cock.

'Isn't it a lovely necklace?' Philip asked.

'I could have spent the whole evening admiring it,' Rob admitted.

'Why don't you take another look?' Sophie suggested. 'Philip and I can go and get fresh drinks for us all from the bar.' She turned to Philip and said, 'You don't mind giving me a helping hand, do you, Philip? We can discuss that job vacancy you mentioned.'

He was standing and beside her in a moment. She was pleased to see that he stood awkwardly, clumsily disguising his erection as he hurried to keep up with her. She walked briskly towards the bar, confident he would be close behind her. And she had no hesitation in stepping into the Gents toilets before they reached the bar.

Philip followed her.

She dragged him into a cubicle. Slamming the door closed behind them, she pushed herself into his embrace. His body was as lean and hard and as muscular as she had imagined it would be. When his mouth met hers she realised she was being kissed by that lazy, dangerous smile that had already turned her insides into fluttering, horny butterflies.

There was no need for words.

It was easier to simply let their actions do the talking.

She pushed her hands beneath his jacket, taking in the contours of the muscles beneath his shirt. He had a broad chest. His biceps were huge and bulging. As she moved her hands to his back, then down to his buttocks, she thought the muscles felt like steel beneath the skin.

The idea made her yearn for him with renewed force.

At the same time as she explored his body, Philip was pawing at her breasts through the thin cotton of her blouse.

She pressed into him, desperate to feel more.

Unconsciously, she bucked her hips forward and rubbed the mound of her sex against his leg. The friction was deliciously satisfying. She wanted to rub harder and more vigorously but the confines of the cubicle didn't allow for much movement.

Her hand snaked to his groin. She unzipped his trousers with a practised flick of her wrist and then her fingers were closer to freeing his erection. He wore no pants and she immediately touched the bare skin of his cock. The length seemed satisfyingly thick and pleasantly long. She stroked her hand back and forth along him, enjoying the way her caresses made his kisses more ferocious.

'I came prepared,' she murmured.

She held up the emergency rubber from her purse.

He grinned and nodded. 'Is that my size?'

'Shall we try it on and find out?'

As she ripped the condom from the packet, Philip's fingers disappeared between her thighs. She shivered as he caressed upwards with determined urgency. And then she held herself still as he pressed his touch against the crotch of her panties. There was a thin layer of cotton separating her sex from the skin-on-skin touch of his fingers against her wetness.

The nearness of that intimacy was enough to make her shiver.

She had been excited before but now she was so close to climax that teasing was almost painful. Her breath came out in ragged sighs. Her chest heaved and fell in soft, agonised shards. She met the steel of his gaze and tried not to be thrilled by the cruelness of his cool smile.

He rubbed a finger against the centre of her cotton-covered crotch.

She bristled.

Gently, he stroked another finger against the side of her panties, stroking the bare skin at the top of her thighs. Although Sophie had no way of seeing what he was doing, she could mentally envision the movement of his finger sliding against the soft flesh. She suspected his touch was lubricated by her perspiration and the moisture from the centre of her crotch.

Then he was peeling the panties aside.

She moaned.

15

It felt as though her damp gusset was kissing goodbye to her moist labia. The movement of the fabric caressed her sex with a cooling balm of fresh air.

Urgently, Sophie rolled the rubber over Philip's erection. As soon as it was in place she tugged him between her thighs and guided the tip of his thick length to her sex. Trembling, she nestled her lips over him and then met his gaze again.

Philip was still smiling.

Bracing herself for the pleasurable thrill of his penetration, Sophie slowly lowered herself on to his cock.

They both groaned. She rode swiftly up and down on him, wanting to make the moment stretch out for an age, but knowing that this would only be a rushed and delightfully satisfying quickie. The lack of glamour in their surroundings, and the lack of comfort in having to have sex while standing, was working against her. But, rather than complain about the conditions, Sophie figured she would take as much from the experience as she could.

She squeezed her inner muscles tight around him and savoured the climactic thrill of the pleasure flooding through her body. In the same moment, as the orgasm shattered through her body, Sophie felt Philip's erection pulse deep inside her sex.

She pushed him away as soon as his cock had stopped throbbing. 'You go and get the drinks from the bar,' she told him. Reaching down to his diminishing erection, she snatched the condom from him and said, 'I'll dispose of this and freshen up before I come back.'

He nodded. And then he was gone.

Sophie waited until she'd heard the door of the Gents close before she left the cubicle and went to the bathroom mirror. She dropped the used condom into a convenient waste bin and then checked her reflection.

Her heartbeat was pounding furiously.

The encounter had been sufficiently brief so that it hadn't upset her clothes or her make-up. A veneer of perspiration covered her brow and her cleavage but that could have been dismissed as effects of the stifling African heat.

Deliberately, she unfastened her blouse and then refastened it with one button in the wrong place. It was a sign she had often used with Rob to surreptitiously tell him that she had been playing with someone else. Satisfied with the way she looked, Sophie rushed out to join Philip and maintain the pretence of normalcy.

'The barman was a little slow,' she explained as she and Philip rejoined Rob and Angela at the table.

'As long as he got the order right this time,' Angela said. 'I ordered a dirty martini before and it wasn't very dirty.'

'And you like it dirty?' Rob asked with feigned innocence.

Angela flashed a sour smile at him. 'I love my martinis

17

to be dirty. Yes.' She looked set to say something more and then noticed the misaligned buttons on Sophie's blouse.

'Look at these,' she said, encouraging Sophie to step closer. 'Let me sort them out for you.'

Sophie swallowed and did as Angela asked.

The blonde worked with deft speed, teasing the buttons through their holes and then refastening them. Her fingers rested against Sophie's tingling skin with a lightness of touch that was like the most intimate of lover's caresses. As she was adjusting the clothes, Sophie realised it would be great to spend the night with Philip and Angela because she believed either member of the couple would be equally satisfying as a playmate.

'There you go,' said Angela, patting Sophie's chest. 'You're properly dressed now and looking lovely again.'

Sophie glanced at Rob and nodded tersely. They didn't usually do much in the way of silent communication and this was as close as it came to them trying to communicate psychically. She wanted him to invite Philip and Angela to spend the night in their suite. She wanted them to stop pretending that none of them knew swinging existed and she wanted them all to go upstairs, get naked and fuck.

Rob seemed to understand what she was saying.

He cleared his throat and then glanced from Angela to Philip. 'You'll have to forgive me for being so straightforward,' he began. 'But I'm curious to know. Do you two play?'

'Play?' asked Philip uncertainly.

'Swing,' Sophie interjected. 'Do you two swap? Do you two share?'

Her voice trailed off as she realised she was running out of synonyms and neither Angela nor Philip was making any move to show they knew what she was talking about.

'Rob and I have an open relationship and we were wondering if you two had a similar understanding?'

Philip and Angela exchanged a glance. Angela looked momentarily panicked. Philip soothed her with a comforting pat on her wrist.

'No,' Philip told Rob. 'We don't swing or play. We're totally monogamous in our relationship.'

He shot a warning glance at Sophie. At the same moment Sophie noticed that Angela was flashing a similar warning glance at Rob.

'Although,' Philip continued, 'I'm sure I speak for Angie as well as myself when I say we're both very flattered by your interest.'

'But ...' Rob started.

Sophie clutched his leg. 'Isn't that sweet, Rob?' she said, speaking over her husband. 'Perhaps we should practise monogamy like Phil and Angela and see how that works out for us?'

He nodded and placed his hand over the one she had
on his leg. In a soft voice, too soft for either Philip or
Angela to hear, he said, 'We already do practise monogamy
like Phil and Angie. I owe you a grand.'

Four For The Seesaw
Charlotte Stein

'Go on, Tia,' he says, and I want to say no. But he's rubbing and teasing my nipples – which are tight and swollen anyway – and it's real muggy and close in here, and I don't know. Why would I want to say no, again?

He knows that I like what he's doing. He sticks out his tongue and wets the material of my T-shirt, pushing that slickness down and down through the material until it's all over my stiff nipple. And then he licks and sucks the tip until I'm squirming on the airbed, glancing across at the sleeping forms of Sean and Kay.

They're going to wake up. It's obvious they're going to. I'm not a quiet fucker and we're only in this tiny little tent.

I spread my legs open for him anyway. He gives me

this cheeky grin when I do, before getting his hand right down there to rub and worry my clit. I'm already really wet, so his fingers just slide around in all my juice, easing down to my grasping hole before coming back up to rub me some more.

Any second I'm going to come. I'm going to come in a tent with our friends right there next to us, and I'll be really loud and probably say dirty stuff like *fuck my cunt*.

When he slides down, down into the tight heat of our shared sleeping bag – that smirky smile still on his cheeky lips – I hiss at him no. No, God no. I fight against him in the strict confines of the sleeping bag, but he's between my legs before I know it. He just tugs my knickers aside and runs his tongue along the length of my slit, all over the plump outer lips, and then worms inside to find my stiff bud.

I know why he's doing this. I do. It's all because I confessed that I think Sean's a real cutie, and he confessed that he thinks Kay's a babe, and everything is now going downhill from there. At the top of the hill are normal people, who get jealous when their other halves talk about how hot someone else is. At the bottom there's us, trying to get off with our objects of desire right next to us.

I bite my lip hard and glance across at them. Both of them are still sleeping, but that doesn't help me all that much. They're so pretty to look at and this is such a filthy thing, that it only gets me closer to coming. Sean's got this sexy mouth, real soft and sensual with lips that hardly seem to have any outline. And his eyelashes are like a girl's, fanning out soft and charcoal black against his milky skin.

Ryan thinks he's too feminine, but that's not true. He's got a real masculine air about him, what with the strong jaw and his jutting chin. His blue eyes go right through you, and it almost makes me wish they were open, now.

Almost.

And, oh God, Kay's lovely, too. I can see what Ryan likes about her. That great big thick swatch of red hair, that cupid's bow mouth. I bet a mouth like that looks amazing sliding down Sean's cock, while he arches up on the bed for her. I bet he arches. I bet they look so good together, what with her being so small and slight and him so big.

And then Ryan catches the underside of my clit with just a flick of his tongue, and I forget whatever it was I'd been thinking. The trembles my body is going through spiral suddenly out of control, and a tense, tight orgasm grabs holds of me – one that makes me jerk and groan and cream all over his face, picturing Sean's mouth pressing against Kay's sex. His tongue in her pussy, circling her clit.

God, that's good.

It's so good that I don't stop Ryan when he climbs back over me, and notches the head of his cock against my slippery hole.

'My turn now,' he says as he shoves in, and I notice that he can't stop his eyes straying over to Sean and Kay, either. Ah, the grass is always greener. Though I suspect the grass is meant to stay green and over there. Not right in our faces as we fuck an inch away from it.

'I love you,' I tell him, as he drives into me. 'I love you.'

But I'm staring at Sean's sleeping face as I say it.

We're being far too loud, and I suppose I shouldn't be surprised when Sean opens his eyes. Though I am just the same, and even more so because I'm looking right at him when he does it. He seems startled to see me so close and intent on him, but then that's how he is. A little nervous, a little uptight.

I'm sure he's going to get tighter still when he realises what we're doing.

I don't shy away, and so I see him studying me close up. His eyes inch over the rutting shapes we make slowly, in sections: first flicking to the place where our joined hips will be, beneath the sleeping bag. Then to Ryan's hand over mine, on the pillow. Then back to my face, still turned towards his.

I've always loved the way Sean shows interest in things. By careful, studious increments, as though his eyes are better able to explore something than his hands. There's an aloofness about him, too, as though even something as base as sex is a thing you can detach yourself from and examine.

He isn't like Ryan at all. Ryan is quick witted and open, he's bold. Sean hangs back, assessing, first. His assessing makes me flutter the muscles of my pussy around Ryan's cock, and he grunts when I do.

I want to ask Sean, *Do you ever grunt?* But just the idea of asking him something like that makes me twist beneath my thrusting boyfriend, clit sparking, nipples tense, the tight coils of another orgasm winding up low down deep in my belly.

I close my eyes tight against it, but when I open them again Sean is still watching with those strange curious eyes.

'Kiss him,' Ryan says, and I almost jump at the rude intrusion of his voice into something that had momentarily seemed so private. As though he's just a machine, over me, servicing me, while I gaze at something pretty.

But Sean just gives him an incredulous look. I think he believes Ryan is kind of a jerk. But then so am I, because I'm doing this too. Right? And if he wants to think that, well he can go ahead, and have something for his trouble, too –

I lean forward as quick as anything, and plant one on him.

His eyes stay open when I do it, but he doesn't try to push me away. He just lets me press my lips to his, and, when he stays that passive while I slide my tongue into his mouth, I moan. Thick pleasure gushes through me and I come just like that, Ryan's cock working in me and my wet mouth on Sean's, Ryan groaning like a loon as he follows me.

I make my sounds right into Sean. I come in his mouth, so to speak.

He doesn't seem to mind all that much. I think I make rather a nice specimen for him to examine and assess. I'm an interesting experiment, one that leaves a pleasing flush on his cheeks.

And when he asks me: 'Was that good, Tia?' I almost come all over again.

***

I suspect Kay knows. She's not exactly angry with me for coming in her boyfriend's mouth, but she keeps looking at me sly. As we're hiking through the woods, as we're looking out over the lake and taking pictures, as we're buying tourist crap from Ye Olde Gift Shop.

When Sean stands next to me and gives his opinion on the snow globe I'm thinking of buying, she looks at me even slyer. He puts his hand on my shoulder. She puts her hand on Ryan's arm.

It's all very car keys in the big bowl.

I look up at Sean, but his face is as unreadable as always. He could be thinking about fly faeces, for all I know. That's what Ryan whispers in my ear as we leave the shop – that all day and all night Sean's head is filled with thoughts of bugs and the things that bugs do and giant bug orgies. I can't argue with him, because Ryan sat in on Sean's seminar on the secret lives of bees or whatever, and I didn't.

But what I can't tell is this: is my wicked tongue-forever-in-his-cheek boyfriend trying to make me want Sean more, or less? He knows I love all that Professor Kinsey stuff, all that rigorous scientist researching bedroom habits nonsense. After he came back from the lecture I had said to him: *Tell me. Tell me all about it. Tell me what Sean said and how he said it.*

And then he told me, on the bed and on the floor and in the shower.

'Knock it off,' I snap at him, and give him a shove.

But he won't knock it off. When we're all in the lake together, mostly just in our underwear and sliding around each other beneath the veil of the water, he pulls me close and kisses me, and kisses me. Our legs tangle together and I can feel he's stiff as anything, right up against my belly and begging for attention.

And then he murmurs in my ear: *I bet he's hard too, just thinking about your face when you come.*

Mostly all I can hear and feel is the water lapping up against me, cold against the places the sun is trying to warm, and then the hot brand of Ry's erection, and then the hot push of his breath against my ear and my throat. I glance across at Kay and Sean as they splash near the shore, and he keeps right on whispering.

'I imagine fucking her,' he tells me. 'While thinking about you.'

He's always so honest, so honest that I can hardly stand it. I free his hard-on from his shorts even as they get closer, fondling the swollen shaft just a little, just enough to get him to hide his face in my shoulder. And then I wrap my legs around his waist and slide my own underwear aside, so that I can ease down on him while I watch them frolic.

Kay, in her little red boy shorts and Sean all lean and strong. We hide it well, I think, but when he looks our way I know he knows. He knows well before Ryan grabs the side of my face and presses his mouth hard into the curve of my throat, his cock ploughing a possessive furrow through my ever-molten pussy.

Though I'm not sure how possessive it really is, all of this crazy, frantic sex. It seems so much more like we've all crossed our arms over each other's, and no one knows who's hand they're really holding any more.

* * *

It's like a puzzle game. A sort of jigsaw. Tonight Kay is sleeping on the inside and Sean is at the tent wall, as though she's trying to protect him from something. And yet another piece has shifted into a different position too, so maybe she's not so protective after all. She just wants to lie next to Ryan, while I lie like a bookend to Sean – against my tent wall, too.

I suppose I should feel shut out and bereft, but I don't. I want to go to sleep as quickly as possible, so that he can secretly kiss her in the night. Then we'll be even; then the puzzle will be complete. One of each, car keys in the bowl.

Though I know that I don't want to stop at one of each.

I glance across at Ryan's face, beside me on the pillow. He looks boyish when he's asleep, and in the dim golden glow of the battery-powered lamp we've kept on, even more so. Innocent, I guess you could say – though he's anything but. He's my cheeky imp, my sweetest thing, my giver of many gifts. Some of them sexual, some of them not.

I touch his face and he makes a little snuffling noise – a silly noise, that tells me he's only half-asleep. Then he sneaks his hand up from inside the sleeping bag, and clasps his fingers around mine. Just right there against his cheek.

I'm almost afraid to go to sleep, in case I wake up to

him making love to another woman. But then again, what if I stay awake and he doesn't? What if later on down the line we hate each other for never letting us be the people we didn't know we wanted to be? Tia with a scientist, Ryan with an actress.

You've got to swap and change and explore and find out about your body with another completely different sort of body, while you still can. I remember saying to him: *What sort of person would I be if I had never met you?*

Better, he had said. But I don't think that's true.

I go to sleep, with my hand still in his.

***

I wake up to sighs, and moans. Soft and faint, as though knowing they have to hide. Automatically I think of Ryan and Kay going at it, and for a moment I'm afraid to open my eyes. Even though I maybe possibly wanted this, I'm afraid, I'm afraid. All those conventional feelings that he'd probably mock well up in me: what if he likes her better, what if I don't want him to like her better, what if I don't really want Sean at all so it's not OK for him to like Kay?

But when I open them, Ryan has his head in the pillow. Utterly asleep and oblivious.

It's Kay and Sean who have the reins of whatever

sleigh ride we're on. Or rather, Kay does. She's the one calling the shots, and her shots are these:

'They did,' she's whispering. 'Why can't we?'

And then she gives out a faint little moan, because I guess whatever she's doing to herself feels nice. It's certainly not anything that Sean's doing to her, because he looks tense and tight and is lying ever so slightly off to one side, and when he speaks it's in a straining sort of voice.

'Because we're not like them,' he says, and I wonder what he means. Not like the sort of person who screws in a lake, or while lying next to other people? Because I wasn't either, before I met Ryan. And I suspect Kay isn't much either, while she's with Sean.

Though I gather she'd kind of like to be.

'Come on,' she says. 'Just shove it in me.'

Yeah. I kind of think she might.

'I know you're hard.'

'That's irrelevant,' he says, but then she reaches down to the place where said hardness will be, and he flinches as though struck.

'No-oo-oo,' he whines, and then in a sterner sort of voice: 'I can't in front of other people.'

Though I really don't think that matters so much, when she's already got her eyes closed and is definitely playing with herself. She doesn't say it, but the meaning's clear: if you won't, I will.

It's just as she gets her hand underneath the clingy vest she's wearing to play with one of her spiky little nipples as she squirms and sighs, that he looks away exasperated and catches me looking back. Only then does his face flush. Though I don't think he's embarrassed because his girlfriend is masturbating while I watch. I don't think he's embarrassed that he's probably got an erection, either.

I actually think it might be because he's the one hanging back. He's the one with a lack of daring. His girlfriend is willing to get herself off in front of other people, and I'm the girl who fucked her boyfriend and kissed his pretty mouth while I did it.

Sean, on the other hand, is capable of nothing. Just a boring scientist set in his boring conventional ways.

He glances down at Kay, her eyes scrunched tight shut and her mouth a cute round O as her fingers work on whatever they were working on, and then his eyes seem to darken. He doesn't look cross exactly, but he doesn't look pleased either, and, though it's a surprise to Kay to find him suddenly on top of her, it doesn't surprise me.

He kisses her hard and she squeals into his mouth – I guess he's not usually the sort to be rough. Usually I bet he's restrained, tender, not quite letting himself go. But he certainly seems to be letting something go now.

He yanks her hands out from inside the sleeping bag and pins them above her head, and a strange sort of echo floods over me. I remember the first time Ryan and I screwed – when we'd fallen asleep together one too many times, and I couldn't help looking at his face while I touched myself. He had woken up just as I got too excited to hold back, and then he'd taken me in much the same fashion as Sean is about to take Kay: on my back, hands suddenly and startlingly pinned above my head.

His voice in my ear: *Yeah, I think I'll just finish you off.*

There's something about the scene before me that's the reverse of that, however. It's Kay who pants at him to *do it, do it, yes, fuck me.* Sean seems aggressive with her, but resistant somehow at the same time. His expression only relaxes when he's clearly between her legs and feeling her spread for him – her soft pouting cunt probably slippery with arousal, just aching for the thick push of his cock.

It isn't hard to imagine at all. I'm aching for it too, and it only gets worse when he starts rocking over her and she starts wailing – and, dear God, does she ever. She cries and pants and moans and claws at him while he keeps up this steady solid rhythm – almost as though he's insensible to her reaction. The only clue that he's enjoying himself is the spreading flush on his cheeks and the way he's biting at his lower lip, but somehow that just makes him more alluring.

I wonder what it would take to crack through that

façade. Certainly not all the groaning and squealing that Kay's doing. She looks a picture: cheeks hot pink, eyes closed, lips gleaming and open. And the words she babbles – *yes, right there oh yes, baby, you're doing it, oh fuck my little pussy* – are arousing even to me. But I guess that's not enough for the man of science.

She comes long before he does. I know she does, because she pants *kiss me now, now*, and I take my eyes off Sean long enough to realise that Ryan is awake, and she's talking to him. She must have known what I did with her boyfriend, and now she wants some of the same – she wants Ryan to kiss her as she comes.

Which he does. And not to my consternation, but certainly to Sean's.

He moves back a little to let it happen – not that he has much of a choice – but I can see the dazed hurt clear on his face. He swipes a hank of hair off his forehead and pulls completely away from her when she doesn't end the kiss with her orgasm, and then he just sits back on his heels, sleeping bag swaddled around all the parts I want to see, watching his girlfriend make out with my boyfriend.

He doesn't see it as a free pass, the way I do. He just looks hurt and confused.

Or, at least, he does until he turns his gaze back to me.

I pull away from Ryan and sit up, gazing right back

at Sean with steady eyes. Even in the low light I can see there's a faint gleam of sweat on his upper lip and at his temples, and that he's trembling just a little. With tension, I think – the tension of whatever it is we're doing, and the tension of not getting that orgasm he clearly needs.

I know he hasn't come without seeing a lick of evidence. It's obvious. And yet he still goes rigid when I clamber over my boyfriend's body to get at him.

For a second I'm sure he's not going to take whatever I'm about to offer. Or at least I think so before he lays that assessing look on me, as I crawl across the tent towards him. The light in his eyes flickers and dances, and he leans down, breathless, when I move up to kiss him.

I don't let our lips touch, however. I ghost them over his until he's clearly caving and then I back away, just a little. Ryan used to do the same to me, all the time – just be such a fucking tease until I ran river-wet and greedy for him.

And it has the desired effect on Sean. He doesn't make a peep when I curl my fingers under the hem of his sweatshirt, and tug it upwards. He just lifts his arms and lets me pull it off, as though it's a relief to be free of the thing.

Which I guess it must be, with the heat in here reaching apocalyptic proportions, and his cock pointing up the way it is doing. It stands stiff and straight and still glistening with Kay's juices, resentfully red and swollen at the tip. A bead of pre-come wells in the slit, begging for me to lick it up.

In fact, his whole posture begs for me to lick it, in truth. He seems to be holding his breath, and his lips are parted as though suggesting what he wants me to do.

And thankfully for him, I'm not one to say no. In fact, in this case I don't even have to say anything at all. I just part my lips and poke my tongue out, then wait to see if he can be as weak as most people are when they're hot and aching and about ready to pop.

Ryan bet me he would be. Turns out he was right.

Sean bumps his hips forward just a little bit – barely enough to be noticeable, but noticeable enough when you're burning for it. And I reward him with a swipe of my tongue all the way around the head of his cock, following that neat and very pronounced little ridge from start to finish.

He appreciates my wet tongue enough to grasp for more of it, when I back away. His hips rock forward just a tiny bit, and then he's in my mouth – not quite fucking it but clearly wanting to.

It doesn't take long to get him to give in, however. I just tease him a little, barely sucking and only letting him feel the flicker of my tongue occasionally. Never giving him more than I have to, until he's shaking and clenching his fists at his sides.

But even better comes when I palm his tight, swollen balls and he can't seem to stop himself lurching forward. Cock suddenly shoved deep in my mouth. Something like a gag welling up inside me.

I have to lay my hands on his taut and trembling thighs to calm him, but it seems like he doesn't want to be calmed now. He's definitely making little gasping sounds and his cock is leaking steadily. Every time I swirl my tongue around the swollen tip I can taste the tang of his pre-come.

But he still doesn't go over. He doesn't go over when I get my hand around the base of his shaft and rub in time with my working mouth, or when I suck hard while wriggling my tongue against that sensitive spot on the underside, the one that always makes Ryan shoot.

Though the sounds he's making definitely get louder. Little desperate groans and sighs that get shakier and shakier – oh, I could live for those sounds. Ryan's got a delicious potty mouth but Sean, God. I've never heard anyone seem so desperate to come, or seen someone so urgent and shaky with it.

It makes my clit swell and my pussy cream. Something which becomes clearer when someone runs a hand over my ass, before pulling the strip of my knickers to one side in order to get a finger in my pussy.

I don't even look back to see who's doing it. I'm just grateful that they are, and more so when they add a second finger alongside the first.

Feels amazing. Feels like something huge against my tender swollen flesh, exciting beyond belief in a way I can't describe. For a brief delirious moment I think of those words I said to Ryan, of what I would have been if I'd never met him, and then I think of nothing else as I recognise his big hands on my hips.

He doesn't ask or say a word. He just drags my knickers down my thighs until they make a chain around my knees, and then while I've got another man's cock in my mouth he pushes his own into my cunt.

I groan loudly around Sean's flesh, and he answers me in kind. In fact, we all echo each other, one after the other, like some sort of unholy round of verse singing. Even Kay joins in, as she watches with big fascinated eyes.

After all, I'm sure she won't be only watching by the end of the night. She'll have my boyfriend panting over her, his cock slick and sliding in and out of her the way it's doing inside me, right now.

Though it won't be the last time for her, even if it's definitely going to be for me. I know it. I can feel it, over and around this thing we're doing.

This is the last time he's going to hook his hands into the curves of my hips, and tug me back on his eager prick; the last time he's going to put one big hand on my back to steady me; the last time I'm going to hear him tell me *harder. Fuck back on me harder.*

Because I don't obey him. I'm not greedy for his cock

– I'm greedy for Sean's. I'm impatient for Sean's orgasm, sucking and licking and pawing him in places he's embarrassed about me going. When I dig my nails into his firm round ass cheeks, he sways like someone drugged. He stutters out a *no, don't*, when I do what Ryan taught me to – slide my hand back around and worm a finger to that soft smooth stretch of skin behind his balls, and press and rub until he's quaking.

Oh, there are so many things I'm going to teach Sean. He's ripe for my tutorials: pressing against his perineum just as he's struggling to come, a slick finger in his ass to make him squirm and blush, stopping and starting and teasing and starting again to make his orgasm extra lush.

My orgasm is going to be extra lush too. Especially when Sean groans that he thinks he's going to come, and Ryan tells him *no, wait.*

Ladies first.

And then he fucks into me hard until all I can hear is the firm wet slap of his thighs against my ass, the thick head of his cock butting against just the right place over and over. One long finger pressing firm to my clit, until I cry around this mouthful of flesh.

'God, you made her come just like that,' Kay says, in the breathy voice of someone newly infatuated.

But she's not wrong. My clit swells against his rubbing finger and the tingles already threading through me grow until they're fit to burst. And then he says *that's it, baby, come on*, and I obey like always. I suck hard and eager on Sean's prick and shudder from head to toe.

Of course the moment I do, Sean cries out. His hand goes to the back of my head and he urges his cock as deep as it will go, spurting over my tongue warm and thick. I remember the first time I ever went down on Ryan and he babbled on through the whole thing – how good and hot my mouth was and how – *oh Jesus* – he was going to do it in my mouth.

But I think, for Sean, even the sound he made and all that grasping of the back of my head was a lot. Coming in front of people he's not dating is a lot. Everything's a lot. And I'm pretty sure Ryan knows that too, because his next words are like he's read my mind.

'See,' he says, as he strokes my back. 'She likes it when you talk to her.'

And there's such a strange fondness in his voice, a warmth that's unlike anything I've ever heard from him. I suppose I should be offended that he's talking over me, that I'm *she*, and yet I'm not. I want to say to Kay the same thing: be good to him. He likes it when you spoon up against his back.

He likes it when you suck him long after he's spent, and he likes taking baths together. He likes fingers in his mouth when he's having sex, and blindfolds are his kink of choice.

Though, in truth, I don't know if I want to say. I know

so well that he likes all of those things, but maybe I won't tell you, Kay. Find out your own things. Could be that they're different. I certainly intend to find out what's different about Sean, all on my own.

Already there's something different. He doesn't want to kiss me with a mouth full of his come. But he does want to spoon against *my* back, and bury his face in my hair, and so it is that I get to lie there and watch, as Kay finishes off my once-was-boyfriend.

It's been a year and a day since I last saw Ryan. I know it has, because Sean tells me as we're driving up to the campsite. Number three thousand and eighty-five on the list of things I've learned about Sean in a year: he's very good at timekeeping. Ryan was always awful at remembering days – he'd throw me three birthday parties a year to make up for the one he forgot.

'Is your mind somewhere else?' he asks, as we come to the turn-off.

'Not really,' I reply, but I'm lying. It is. Currently my mind happens to be on why I still compare Sean to Ryan, even after all this time. It's something I think about a lot lately.

'Nervous about seeing your ex?' he asks, and he does it in that faux-jovial way he has when he's nervous or trying to be someone he's not. He thinks people want humour, lightness, not his crazy intensity.

And maybe they do. Maybe they do. Some people do, some of the time.

'No,' I say, even though I can feel my heart fluttering against its cage.

I don't know why it's doing that. There weren't any heartbroken arguments, no awkward goodbyes. We jiggled the puzzle around – all four of us, even Sean.

In the morning, Ryan had just said to me: *You going with him, then?*

And I had replied: *Sure.*

And then all of our things in swapped-around cars, Kay giggling: *This is crazy! This is crazy! I love it!*

What's in all of that to make me nervous? I've always wondered if Sean felt odd about leaving Kay just like that, but even the thought of him secretly continuing to love her all this time doesn't make me nervous. I don't think he did, anyhow. He told me once that he had never felt the need to say it to her, and if you don't say it …

Ryan used to say it all the time. It never lost its meaning, either, which I guess is pretty odd.

When I see him at our usual camping spot on the hill, I think about him saying: *You really like Sean, huh? You like that whole weird repressed scientist schtick he's got going on. Yeah, I can see it in your eyes. I can see it when you look at me.*

And I had said: *no, no. No, never when I look at you.*

42

Just as we pulled into the campsite, where Sean and Kay were waiting.

* * *

He's almost the same. Wearing the same clothes – goofy T-shirt, smart trousers, hair at odd angles, unshaven.

Kay's not the same. She's all creased up and pissed as hell, and the first words he says to me are: *I cracked wise.* And then he shrugs – yeah, that's Ryan. He'll say something and offend the shit out of someone and then shrug.

Only later, I think at her. *Later, he'll come to you with hot chocolate or a Kinder egg or something else suitably ridiculous, and tell you how much he didn't mean it.*

It's just the way he is. It's a defence mechanism, a shield for his tender insides. A test, to see if you honestly and really do love him and can put up with his craziness.

But she doesn't stop being pissed all through putting up the tent and all through dinner, and he doesn't bring her a present. Maybe that was just for me. Something completely different to how he acts with any other person, just for me.

I bet with other people he never said sorry.

* * *

I wake up in the middle of the night with Sean's mouth pressed to the turn of my throat. I guess he's come a long way since we started this whole thing, because that may just be his erection rutting against my thigh.

I smile at him through the darkness, and he looks at me all sweet and eager – so much more open now. Cheeky, even. A little more sure of himself, too. He even talks to me when we fuck, halting words that don't quite reach sexy.

But they're good just the same.

I let him tug my pyjama bottoms down, and climb over me. I'm already wet, of course, though he doesn't seem surprised to find me so. Sometimes he is, as though he can't imagine why I've been thinking about sex.

But I think he knows why I've been thinking about it now.

He gets on over me, even so. He slides into me, slow and easy. And I try to only watch him, I really do. I press my hands against his ass and work my hips up at his, chasing the syrupy pleasure until my tight nipples are fizzing with it and I'm so slippery that it trails down between my ass cheeks.

Though I know it's not enough.

'Talk to me,' I say to him, but the words he manages are not enough either.

It's a good thing, really, that Ryan's there to provide them for him.

'All this time,' he says. 'And you never told him how hard you like it?'

I glance across at him and he's just lying there, head on his pillow, expression soft and innocent. He's a little amused, I think, though not cruelly so.

'Go on,' he says to Sean. 'Give it to her hard. Really fuck her – she loves getting fucked.'

I bite my lip and try to turn away from him. I try to pretend that Sean jolts hard against me because he wants to, and not because Ryan has put something in the suggestion box. But he has, and oh there's plenty more where that came from.

'You know what else she likes? When you gasp for her, nice and high. As though her pussy is the sweetest, hottest, wettest bliss you've ever felt around your cock. As though she caught you j-u-ust right, and now you're thinking of every boring thing you can to hold off that almighty orgasm.'

I can't stop looking at him. I don't think Sean can stop himself, either.

'And you're the authority,' he says, in his best man-of-science voice, but Ryan seems unfazed. He doesn't even look away from me to meet what I'm sure is Sean's accusatory stare.

'No, not the authority. It'd take years and years to puzzle someone like Tia out. But I'll give you one more free tip.' He leans in close, so close that he almost puts

Sean off his stride. 'If you get her as she's about to come, and she's shaking in just that way she is now, and you cover her mouth with yours – she'll give it up, just like that. Right ... into ... your mouth.'

And then he kisses me, he kisses me, he kisses me.

Of course, he's right. I come so hard that my body arches up off the bed, and he has to hold me down. Not Sean – Ryan. Ryan puts his big hands over my shoulders and I buck against them, long waves of sensation rolling up my body and out of my mouth, to pour into him.

Always into him.

And I think: you knew. You always knew. You let me fly away to far and different distant shores, just so that I could turn around again, and fly right back to you.

Dirty Reunion
Scarlet Rush

You asked me if I remembered that night at Tabitha's party. The one where I caught Michael kissing and groping our flirty hostess. Where I ran off to the toilet for a cry, but instead somehow ended up with your stiff cock in my hand. I replied that I could barely remember twenty minutes ago, let alone twenty years, but that was a lie. Actually, I do still clearly remember the illicit exhilaration of holding your erection for the first time, even though the episode is now half my life away. It was the sheer size of you that sent the cold tingle pouring from my belly and into my veins. It was only the second one I had ever seen in the flesh, and I had never considered Michael small in that department. I couldn't tell you but it felt huge in my palm, like a thick slab of warm fillet steak. I tried to imagine it inside me and the thought almost made my legs give way.

You sat me on the side of the bath because I was trembling so much. You had me hold it and stroke it for you, slowly up and down. You had to place your hand on mine to guide me, such was my silent awe for your thickness. Of course, you had pressed it against me many times back when we were girlfriend and boyfriend, but I had never once let it out. It was always safely behind your zip. I had no clue such a monster was concealed. To suddenly grip its full dimensions, with my fingers not even able to meet around it at the middle, was to grasp a reality surely impossible to have ever been unaware of. It was like suddenly discovering that your ex-lover had all the while been a Mafia boss, or a Bourne-style secret agent!

You wanted me to suck it. I remember you broke our kiss and tried to encourage me by pushing upon my shoulder. It was only a slight pressure and I resisted. For some reason, stroking seemed so much less an act of betrayal than sucking. You said I wasn't cheating, even if Michael, my boyfriend of four years since my break-up with you, was at that very party. Yes, the man who would soon become my husband was only a flight of stairs away and yet still you claimed it wasn't cheating. You said I could always invoke the *First Love Rule*. This rule, according to you, meant that you and I could do whatever we wanted with each other, whenever through time we met, and no one could touch us for it. We could be as close as we wanted, as physical as we needed to be, and this couldn't be denied us by anyone, simply because we were each other's First Love. That gave us a special bond, you claimed. Later love might last longer. It might be stronger and truer, but First Love was unique. Your first lover *belonged* to you, forever. That was unequivocal, or so you said.

I remember thinking there must be something to this contrived rule of yours to have me doing what I did. I still couldn't put my mouth upon you. I wanted to. I will tell you that now, since you seem to have stripped away my ability to keep any secrets. Conscience prevented me, even if the only reason I was there was because I caught my supposed boyfriend with his hand inside his own First Love's dress. Because I wouldn't go down on you, I recall you had to stop me and spit on your thumb to smear some lubrication on to your exposed tip. You showed me how to do it and work it in with your foreskin. Then you made me spit on my thumb too, to add to it. Looking back, it was just plain dirty, but at the time it felt tender. I guess that must have been due to our 'Special Bond'!

You wanted to slide your fingers down into my knickers, but I said no.

'I want to put my fingers inside you and have you come all over them,' were your exact words.

That was it with you, always so bluntly rude. When we were together I thought you so big and handsome, so comforting. You were my ever-so-witty man, my clever, strong guardian angel. But you were anything but safe. You were full of wild spirit and wild dreams that both thrilled and scared me senseless. Most of all you were full of hormones, and that is why we couldn't stay together. We split, if you remember, because you wanted to take our physicality to the next level and I disagreed. You dumped me. So it was ironic that four years on, the next time we were alone together, you thought it fine to unashamedly ask to put your hand inside my knickers.

You told me you *had* at long last to be inside me. I just shook my head, even though the pain of not letting you far outweighed the sublime pain that letting you stretch me open would have brought. In the end you just kissed me and held your hand over mine to guide me quicker up and down your pulsing prick. I can't believe I'm using such rude words – see what you've done to me? You made me take you all the way. The memories are still clear. As you neared you moved your hand faster over mine and we got up to blurring speed. I can still see your face, your head going back as you closed your eyes and gasped. I can still vividly recall my own little gasp as I watched the flurry of your hard spurts, the mass of seed shooting out in thick wads with each swift up-stroke. To this day I have never seen so much in one go. It left me shaking and aghast. You would have choked me for sure if I had done your bidding and let you do it in my mouth.

The rest is a grey area and still the subject of our recent chats. I left you there without a single word before you had even zipped yourself back up. The guilt chased me away with my head still throbbing and my cheeks flushed red. I ran down the stairs with my mind jumbled, completely forgetting Michael's earlier errant behaviour that had driven me to you in the first place. I found my boyfriend drinking and chatting away as untroubled as ever and I went straight into his arms. Later you tried to catch my eye but I wouldn't be drawn. In the end you left the party and we didn't speak for twenty years, both it seems fearing each other's ire. You went off to university and I got pregnant and married. You only existed for me in my private moments and I would have all but forgotten you completely if not for the power of social-network websites.

***

It's funny how history is always there, creeping up on you. It just seems to follow you around! It is surely inconceivable that Tabitha Hayden-Smith could still be having such an effect on my life, but this is clearly the case. She was once my archenemy, back when she was just Tabitha Hayden, when she was like a whirlwind passing through our inception into young adulthood. None of us escaped the suck of her vortex. I guess my memories of her differ from yours. All the girls had the daggers out for her, although she knew behind our sneers there was much jealousy. She was the first to lose her virginity, at least a couple of years before the rest of us. She openly declared she was addicted to sex and there was *nothing* dirty she wasn't prepared to do. She flitted from boyfriend to boyfriend and had the best of them queuing up for their turn. She had sex in cars and in dusk-shadowed parks, even on public transport. She admitted to threesomes and alluded to orgies. I remember her saying once that what she most wanted for Christmas was 'a cock in her bum' – and that was in the days when such things were still barely thinkable. She told all of us girls to watch out because she was after our fannies, and she got some of them too. She never quite got mine, but I admit there were a couple of times she gave me the type of melting look that nearly earned her it.

She is still pretty. The years seem only to have made her more alluring. She still has *that* body, that same flawless white skin and those captivating cat eyes. She still has that apparently ever-present wide mischievous smile that reels everyone in. All except for you, that is. You will remember that back when we were an item she made no secret of the fact she wanted you. I lived in constant fear of her poaching you from me. You would smile and tell me there was no chance of this, ever, but it didn't stop the trepidation. I think she targeted you even more because you wouldn't yield like all the rest. You were the trophy she never won.

Michael certainly had his turn, on more than one occasion. You may recall that, while I was with you, he was like her floating boyfriend for a short while, one that didn't mind her flitting off to shag a garage mechanic or a forty-year-old driving instructor before going back to him. He never cared. He has never lost his soft spot for her. It must be down to that First Love thing you keep mentioning, although I'm not sure how much of it was love as opposed to lust in their case. When he became my boyfriend he still thought it OK to cuddle her and grope her bottom whenever they saw each other, no matter that she might be with someone else, and especially no matter that he was supposed to be with me. To this day they have kept in touch. I have no idea what goes on between them in their texts and internet chats and frankly I would rather not know. I just turn a blind eye. It's odd really but I don't mind. Does that sound stupid? I'm just used to Michael being a terrible flirt, and the more he does it, the more secure I feel, because he is *mine*, and he always lets me know this. At the end of the day it is always *me* that gets his unfailing attention and never down the years has this not been the case. If anything, Tabitha's parties brought us even closer together. Oh yes, I haven't quite told you all about Tabitha's other parties, have I?

***

The first came out of the blue, a couple of years back. I had no idea she and Michael were on such close terms to have instigated an invite after such a long time. She apparently has a birthday party each year and for this one she wanted as many of us old faces as possible to turn up. My initial instinct to avoid the party like the plague gradually evaporated. After all, you might be there. I will admit now, and I know you will laugh and consider this a massive triumph, but I had butterflies every day for two months before that party, wondering if you would be there. So imagine the anticlimax when you didn't show! What I haven't yet told you is that there were other climaxes by the end of the night to think about.

Michael must have been very eager to get there as we were the first to arrive. Her house is simply enormous, a proper manor in acres of landscaped grounds. I should have guessed she would never settle for anything less. Being a fashion designer, she decided to greet us wearing one of her own numbers. Being Tabitha, this meant essentially some kind of take on a burlesque dancer's outfit. As you can imagine, this made for an uncomfortable start, what with the history between us and my husband unashamedly gawping at her with his tongue hanging out. Fortunately, Mr Smith showed a bit more decorum. He might sound plain but I have to say he is anything but. Tabitha has done rather well for herself there. He is a decorated army officer, a colonel, no less. He comes from very wealthy stock, hence the house. He is properly posh and rather dishy too, as big as you and with the same dark hair. He was how I pictured you to look now. For one jolting moment I thought she had got one over on me and finally bagged The One That Got Away. Then I remembered that you were far from posh and the least likely person to get a job that meant taking orders from anyone!

Before my husband dissolved into a gibbering heap, decorum reigned and Tabitha decided to leave the boys alone and take me on a tour of the house. I still don't know if she did this to spare my blushes or just to show off her wealth. She seemed genuine enough, but that was Tabitha. In truth she never showed me any animosity and all past frostiness came from my side. She had a knack of behaving like everything was just water off a duck's back. I wanted to hate her but I never really could. She was just too remorselessly open and downright funny. *Bubbly*, people used to call her, but I thought *effervescent* was nearer the mark. There was always an edge to everything she did. I loved her house though – I can't pretend otherwise. She even showed me her best-kept secret, a vast wardrobe with a concealed door in the back, leading not to Narnia, but to a big dressing room complete with a large leather chaise longue. Now, that I did like!

The other guests turned out to be a mix of the old and the new, but not so many of the former. I didn't care. I only really wanted to see you and you weren't there. Michael loved it, of course. He was off to get a closer view of all the plunging necklines and to flirt with as many of the new girls as he could. Tabitha is now in with a very smart and affluent crowd, the type who frequent wine bars rather than pubs. They were all full of the confidence that wealth brings. They were chatty and touchy-feely with one another. They laughed loudly and with genuine mirth. I expected a veneer of nicety over hidden animosity, but I never spotted any. They seemed to be there for one thing only: to have fun.

Tabitha came alive as she always did. The evening was a runaway juggernaut carried relentlessly on by her bawdy character. There was endless drink. No one was allowed to escape having a dance. She twirled around with everyone in turn and grasped inappropriate handfuls as she did so. At one point she put her hands up her skirt and came out holding her lacy black knickers, which she waved around before putting them on her husband's head. She then lined up all the girls in a row and did an impromptu can-can. She delivered it in true Tabitha style, complete with high leg kicks to give us a brief flash under her dress, and an eye-popping, skirt-up, bare-arsed finale.

A 'Smoochiest Slow Dance' competition followed, where pairs of names were drawn blindly to ascertain the partners, who were supposed to then perform as saucily as they could upon the dance floor. All refusals to compete were ignored. Fortuitously I drew the dishy colonel, so it wasn't all bad! I did have to resist like mad when he held me tight and tried to cajole me into kissing him. More shockingly, I had to try to ignore a very noticeable swelling that he was trying to press against me! Tabitha picked one of her delicious new female friends, and not only did they full-on French kiss with absolute commitment, the hostess held her partner's hand and made her slip it up under her dress to hold her naked backside. All this brought great cheers from the clapping ring of spectators around them. They won the competition, obviously. It *was* rather sexy, actually.

Tabitha then gave the rules for her version of Postman's Knock. She seemed intent on having us all kiss each other! Her downstairs toilet was lockable from the outside as well as inside, so she removed the key and passed it in secret for a chosen man to hide on his person. Whenever a girl wished to use the loo she had to go around and kiss the men until she found the one who could produce the key to the door. When she came back she returned the key and the men would secretly swap it among themselves. Any girl who chose to trust to luck and go without the security of the key was deemed 'free for all' and anyone was allowed to get in there with her and do as they pleased. Since there was a lot of drink, there was a lot of peeing to be done and unsurprisingly the men took full advantage of their opportunity. Let's just say there were no quick pecks on the cheek.

The new friends didn't seem to think there was anything odd in all this. It was apparently par for the course with Tabitha. The fact that everyone joined in so enthusiastically made it hard to resist. I witnessed plenty of girls taking much longer than necessary to determine that the key wasn't with the man she was currently embracing. My husband loved the game. I held on for as long as possible and both times I had to go you will be pleased to hear I was lucky to find my target sooner rather than later. I was, however, forced to check with the dishy colonel both times, and I'm afraid to report that his swelling hadn't yet gone down! I'm sure he should have been court-martialled for that.

All these shenanigans were nothing compared to the final, shocking episode. Right at the end of the evening, when a fair few had already finally surrendered and gone home, Tabitha put 'The Stripper' on the CD player and proceeded to prance and wiggle around threatening to perform a full striptease. Her elbow-length gloves came off and she was slowly unbuttoning her lace corset when she suddenly gave up on the idea and grabbed a male member of her watching, grinning audience and tried to coax him into shedding his clothes. She did well, actually. With her help his shirt was soon off. He tried manfully to defend his belt from her busy hands but she got the better of him. His trousers came off and he was left in only his socks and a pair of pristine white cotton Calvin Klein hipsters. I can't say I didn't have a good look, because I did.

She was doing her best *Dirty Dancing* impression, stroking his chest and then grinding her stuck-out bottom into his crotch. I did notice some stretching of the material from within. I thought she was going to complete the job but she pulled her husband into the middle of the circle and started on him instead. The dirty minx had her bottom stuck out into the crotch of the first one while she undid the buttons on her husband's shirt. She wrestled with his trousers and managed to get his zip down but he defended his belt rather better than the first chap and I thought that was that. Then, incredibly, she had her hand back inside his zip and deftly whipped out the colonel's 'little general'! I nearly choked on my wine. She was grinning triumphantly and refusing to let go despite his half-hearted efforts to make her. He seemed just as pleased as she was about the whole thing. In fact, a certain part of him was evidently *very* pleased because it swelled right up in her hand and all she did was release her grip slightly and run her fingers up and down his shaft to ensure the expansion continued. Then there it was, in all its glory, being cheered and whistled and applauded by the crowd. I won't go on about it, but let's just say I've only seen one as big, and we both know who that belongs to.

That wasn't all. Even knowing how brazen Tabitha used to be I never imagined the next bit. Before I had a chance to draw breath she had dropped to her knees and taken her husband into her mouth. It wasn't a performance just for our benefit. It was wanton and hungry, with her sucking hard and slurping noisily while she gripped his shaft and jerked him. Still that was not enough for our naughty friend. She then reached out behind her to catch the first chap's crotch bulge, then rummaged inside his underwear and brought out his cock too. It was easily the most overtly sexual act I had ever witnessed. I thought she was going to do them both but instead she beckoned a girl from the crowd, the one she had earlier smooched with. That girl didn't even bat an eyelid. Into the circle she went and down on her knees. I assumed she was the partner of the other man, but I didn't know for sure. Whatever, she was soon sucking the first chap's cock as avidly as Tabitha was her husband's. It was a slurp spectacular! I didn't know where to look, especially when behind them, in the shadows of a darker corner, I spotted another girl going down on her man. I thought for one moment the whole party would dissolve into a blow-job free for all.

It didn't. Tabitha was suddenly moaning loudly and I quickly deduced that her husband was unloading into her mouth. She kept on going, sucking him dry and then opening her mouth wide in triumph to ensure we all knew his come had been ingested. She turned to see how her friend was faring and the answer was very well. With impeccable timing the first chap was about to let go, but the new girl was less enthusiastic to swallow his spurt and took her mouth away to concentrate on jerking him swiftly to climax. Our delightful friend Tabitha couldn't get out of the way and with a little whoop of surprised joy she found herself having the hot sperm spattered all over her face.

It was a somewhat vulgar if fitting end to their shocking display. I stood there stunned and gawping. I realised I had better shut my mouth quick in case some naughty blighter slipped his prick in it. Around me there was a smattering of applause and some humorous catcalls while the girls hurried off together, presumably to clean up. The two boys stood proudly as they were, slowly zipping themselves back up while they joked with their mates. It was like it was *normal* to them, the standard behaviour for a Tabitha party. I was actually shaking, but the more

I thought about it – and believe me I did a lot of thinking about it over the next weeks – the more it didn't seem out of the ordinary. It seemed wild and thrilling, what adults *should* be doing. Needless to say, Michael loved every second of it. I was surprised he wasn't jealous of the chosen two. The more we talked about it, the more excited he seemed to get about the whole thing. I won't go on about the details, but in time he pretty much admitted that he would have been OK with the party degenerating into a mass oral-sex extravaganza, even if the person I found myself on my knees in front of wasn't him. And that's about the time you came crashing back into my life.

***

I guess internet chats make it so much easier to be forward than a face-to-face meeting, but you rolled back the years instantly with your blunt talk. Once we realised we weren't still harbouring grudges over The Bathroom Incident, you made it your life's work to shock me and get me all hot and horny. You never let my feet touch the ground. You claim I am the prettiest girl you have ever known. You say your one regret in life is never having been inside me. Now that you know I don't harbour any animosity you say you *must* put this right. Within a few months of being back in touch you had me over a barrel. When you are settled as a wife and a mother you don't expect to be suddenly hit by a bolt of passion sent from afar. It is very difficult not to fall for an old flame who fills your head with sexy thoughts and makes you feel like the most desired person alive. You know I can't resist your dirty chat and explicit texts. You know the thrilling naughtiness of it shoots me through with tingling current and brings me alive. You know that deep down I always wanted you and came apart when you left me. My soul always ached for what might have been, despite my happy marriage. You have whittled slowly and surely at my resolve and better nature. You realise I am now a different girl, a naughtier girl, to the one you knew, and you play upon it. You have made me seriously consider doing all the things my marriage vows dictated I wouldn't. You have made me admit all my secrets, even the one about wishing you had been inside me too. Incredibly, because I still can't believe I actually went along with this, you have made me ring you up and ask you, to *plead* with you, to come and fuck me.

In my head I am already a cheat, because of the things I think about and the things I do to myself after our little chats. I fizzle internally for hours after we have spoken and I'm never sure if it's with the excitement of you, or from my guilty conscience trying to shake me free of your spell. Now that the selfish, unreasoned part of my head has decided that you and I must indeed fuck someday, the less treacherous part clings on to some saving graces. First, you have only seen me in recent photos, not in the flesh. Despite your claims that I look better than ever, that you prefer my fuller tits and rounder bottom, this may all go to pot once I strip off and everything hurries downward. I am not the firm-fleshed youth you knew. You say preferences change. You say sexiness is about the person, their character, not their body. If the person is sexy, their body will be too. You live in a dream world! When you are not living there you are living in the Outer Hebrides, for goodness sake! I mean, you may as well be on the moon! And when not living there, you are away on film sets doing your screenwriting. So what chance is there ever, realistically, of you coming all the way down here to meet me? Absolutely none.

* * *

That last assertion has now come back to bite me in the chubby arse, and once again I have Tabitha Hayden-Smith to thank for it. Sneaky Michael has been unable to forget that last party and has been in some secret negotiations with his former love. This year she turns forty and plans the Mother of All Parties. For years she has been building up to this event, testing the water to see which guests are up for it. Michael has been busy assuring her that he and I most certainly are. Without my knowledge he has convinced her that we are prime candidates to have at her Grand Fuck Party, her dirty reunion of all the people she has fucked and wanted to fuck over the years. It is to be a supreme masked ball, a no-speaking, hidden-identity melting pot of shagging couples. Of course, I said no to it. In fact, I kind of *squealed* no to it, such was my surprise that Michael thought we should attend. Then, once he had gone off muttering that we most definitely would be going, I went upstairs and had a wank thinking about it. In my naughty mind all my self-consciousness vanished, along with all the guilt about doing the rudest things with people you have never met. I have to admit, I struggle to find good cause to go against the idea, other than accepted convention that it *must* be wrong. I don't particularly want to have sex with any Tom, Dick or Harry, but the idea of doing it with someone different, without any shame, is rather appealing. I have long since accepted that my husband has a wandering eye, but I never begrudge him this. I am in even less position to do so now that I've spent so much time devoting my rude thoughts to you.

I can't even summon any jealousy over the idea of him and Tabitha together. I know how I feel about the thought of being with you again and it just seems churlish to deny anyone the same. There *is* something to that First Love Rule, you know. It's like, if a love for someone pre-dates that which you have for another, then it remains relevant and legitimate. It's a *different* love to the one you have with your long-term partner, and you can't feel guilty about it because it happened before they came into your life. Listen to me trying to justify your made-up rule! Could this be because you have sworn to get yourself invited to Tabitha's birthday bash?

I know you won't go. Although, during a sneaky peak at Tabitha's Facebook pages (I was trying to deduce who might be attending her Shag Party), I was stunned to see that YOU had recently become her friend. And it seems you have more history with her than you have previously let on. You know she does costume design for the film industry, which I didn't know. Your set-designer girl-friend, it transpires, is a mutual friend. I don't know whether to be annoyed that you never mentioned this before, or excited that it gives you an 'in' to the party. Well, you say you will go, and if there is any possibility you will then so shall I. It could be our one chance in a billion, so perfect it is almost too good to be true. The joke will be on you if you don't show, because everyone, without exception, is expected to join in the naughty fun, and who am I to buck the trend?

***

I think the colonel's hand has been in this because the party is already running like a military operation. You will of course know this if you are already here. The separate invites apparently staggered the arrival time so we didn't all come at once. We must be one of the last here. Having parked in the carriage drive, we were split up immediately by a pair of 'servants'. Two of the converted stable blocks had been designated as the welcome areas, one for the men, the other for the ladies. We changed there. There were racks of costumes provided in all different sizes. Tabitha must have raided the set of some bodice-ripping Jane Austen adaptation to get them all. You gents seem to have been given a running theme of tight riding britches and knee-length leather boots. You are mostly in military uniforms, but I have spotted a couple of highwaymen too. All of you look very dapper, which has helped steady my pounding heart. You have also all been provided with specially produced black fitted eye masks. These are larger than your average Lone Ranger efforts, shaped to go over the nose and cheeks so all but your mouth is covered. Most of us girls were given hand-held masks only, which meant that, while your identities will be kept concealed, ours may not. My mask will stay steadfastly stuck to my face, so, if you are looking for me, I'm the one in the simple wench's outfit, complete with the cleavage that may spill out at any minute.

Our brief was fairly simple. Do not talk to anyone. Go anywhere you please apart from the rooms marked 'private'. Eat and drink what you will. Do what you will, with whoever you choose. Apart from the main hall, if you spend more than ten minutes in any room, you must pair off with at least one of the other occupants – this to thwart mere spectators. All costumes to be returned by midnight, coaches will be waiting outside. That gives me three hours. Looks like my Cinderella moment has arrived. Where are you? I wonder if you have brought your girlfriend or come here in secret. You refused to give me any details in the lead up, just to keep me guessing.

The main hall has been cleared at the centre, with outer tables laden with plates of food and copious amounts of drink. I am on my third champagne and I've barely been here half an hour. I'm sticking here while I get my bearings, assuming you will show eventually. I can't see my husband either. I don't know what he is wearing but I will surely still be able to recognise his demeanour. I've spotted Tabitha. She is unmistakable, even with a covered face. She has allotted herself an ornate fitted glittery gold mask adorned with feathers. She is wearing the tightest under-bosom corset but no other top layer, so her perky breasts are hanging free. Her nipples look just lovely: small and pink and suckable. I cannot believe my husband isn't all over her. Maybe it's because her bottom half consists of leather thighboots and some kind of rubber hot-pant thingies that leave her bottom sticking out, but more importantly have a plastic purple willy built into the front of them. It is thin but quite long, with an upward curve. It doesn't look threatening to me, but it might do to someone as averse to the idea of anal sex as my husband.

Chamber music is playing and some couples are being put through the steps of a period dance by an instructor. Many of the girls have to lower their masks in the process and I can see plenty to please the gents, even with the heavy make-up, presumably to fit the style of the day. Two dances in and I'm wondering how long before the rudeness starts. My answer comes immediately. As the gents line up opposite their partners, Tabitha comes along and one by one undoes the flap of their britches and hauls out their privates. Each man stands with cock and balls on display, in varying stages of readiness. Oh fuck, it's started! To think, by rights I could go and take my pick, take them all if I wanted! They won't know me and vice versa. The thought is mind-boggling and strangely unsettling. I'm feeling way hornier than I imagined and I'm not sure I can trust myself to avoid behaving like an utter whore. I need to find you.

In the drawing room there are a few milling about. Every gent has his flap open and his genitals exposed. I see why the britches were compulsory. We girls may have to show our faces but the men must show more, and that is what ensures the naughtiness. One is standing proud, pointing it right at me. The shaft is wet, like he has just had it sucked. Do I start now or wait for you? Imagine kissing you when I've already had a cock in my mouth. My belly is fluttering and the nerves are giving me pins and needles in my fingers.

To my right, a plump blonde girl is sat alongside a highwayman, her breasts free of her gown. The light nipples have been pinched to hardness. She is bringing his prick up with long strokes. I can see a droplet of pre-come at his tip and she bends down to collect it with a light flick of her tongue. Suddenly she has been hauled across his lap and her gown pulled up. Her bloomers are tight over her fat bum. He aims four, five hard slaps at her with the flat of his hand, to get her squealing. I feel a rush of heat in my puss each time he lands a blow. The gent with the stiff prick points it in their direction. He helps pull down the bloomers so her full expanse of bare arse is on view. Both of them spank her. The pale flesh dances and I let out a gasp. It has all been surreal until this point, but now I *know* I'm in the middle of an orgy. They have stopped spanking her and now have their fingers up her. Imagine – two people with their fingers up you at the same time! I don't know how many, or which holes, but she is wriggling and squealing and pushing her big bum out to get more. The pointy-penis gent stuffs it in her mouth. She is going to get done from both ends and if I stay here any longer they will make me next.

In the study a girl has her gown up and her legs wide open. A hugely bewigged aristocratic woman has her middle finger up the exposed shaven puss. She is taking it out and having the first girl suck on it, then putting it back in and stirring it around. All the while a bare-pricked gent is blowing a stream of cool breath on to the naked fanny. He is fat and small-cocked and I don't want to be used for his dirty pleasure. I hurry out, missing a few doors until I stumble into a billiard room. It has a full-sized snooker table and a roaring fire. Lying upon the table is a lithe, completely naked brunette. She is reclining on one arm and working the fatter end of a cue in and out of her saturated hole, twisting her wrist as she pushes it inside. At either end of the table two gents are frantically serving bent-over wenches from the rear. The furthest one is slapping deep and hard against a juddering chocolate-brown bum. He looks to be trying to drain his aching balls as fast as possible, presumably to get a refill and go on to the next. I'm thinking this gent is Michael. I cannot be sure because he is hunched over her back, but there is just something about his action that I know. He doesn't even look around at me.

I am getting too worked up now. My bloomers feel like I've wet them! I can either give up and take on the next cock I see, or go and get more drink and try to keep on top of the situation. There *is* a cock in front of me but it has been buried inside one girl from the rear, then taken out and slapped around a kneeling wench's face. It's a nice cock too. Should I bend and see if he will do me too? I'm losing my grip. I need a drink. The dancing in the main hall has all but descended into a cock-sucking frenzy. All the girls are at least bare-breasted, one is completely naked and is on all fours, with a lighted candle protruding from her rear end. A couple of the other girls with cocks in their mouths are being licked or fingered from the rear. If I thought the main hall would be a safe haven I was wrong. I must be one of the few girls still fully clothed. It can't last. Someone will spot me and use me. Where *are* you?

It's plain you aren't here, or if you are you are busy elsewhere. I cannot escape the fact that I need someone inside me, I'm just too far gone. The shame of it almost burns. I cannot do it in front of others, so I need to come across a room with only one couple in, or head upstairs and hope a single gent drags me off into a secluded corner. I'm making for the main staircase. Lucky I know the layout of the house so well from my private tour. Oh my God, it's YOU. Up there on the galleried landing. I mean, I think it's you. You are looking at me now so why hasn't your expression changed? Don't you recognise me? You are the first gent to have the flap of his britches still done up. That's a good sign, I suppose. I am getting nearer and getting more convinced it is you. The size of frame is right. The hair colour is right, although I don't

72

know how you style it. You are watching my ascent but giving me no sign. Should I show my face? Shit, Tabitha is there, right behind you. She has her arms around your chest. Don't let me get this close and then lose you to *her*.

She is stroking your front and pulling open your shirt. The torso is lean and the skin smooth and slightly bronzed. Do they even have sun in the Outer Hebrides? Her hand is going down now. She is grasping your crotch and pulling down the flap. I can't breathe. Her hand is inside, gathering as much of you up as she can. She has pulled it all out. I see the darker flesh behind her grasping hand, the smooth fat ball sack hanging down. Now the cock itself is there, growing fast in her grip. It's big, I can see that. I'm trying to remember exactly how big it should be to confirm it is you. She is holding it and gently running her fist along your length. *Spit on it*, I almost blurt out – I *know* you will need some saliva to lubricate the head. The cock is fully hard and huge now. I have still only seen two like it: yours and the colonel's. Oh no – I had forgotten the colonel; the same hair as yours, the same size of body, the same lovely big cock.

Would Tabitha pick her own husband to be with? Maybe she could find no match. But then she wants YOU, I know this. If you were here, she would seek you out. She has always wanted the trophy she never won. Whatever she wants, you are still looking straight at me, letting her tease your shaft but paying her no mind. She is watching me too, with that mischievous smile spread wide. God, she is sexy. I can see why so many fall at her feet. How can I compete with her? Where the hell is my husband to drag her off when I need him? She has let you go and is coming at me, still smiling. She grabs at my front and rips my blouse apart, spilling my breasts out of the tight corset. She has them both, squeezing on them and roughly sucking them in turn. I am close to collapsing. She pulls at my skirt and that is off too. I am now in just my bloomers and corset, staring at you, watching you slowly wank your shaft.

You take my hand and lead me away from her. My legs are so heavy you nearly have to drag me. Many doors are available but you pick one in particular, the one with a note saying 'Private' upon it. I know it is Tabitha's room. My head is spinning because I can't see why you would go against the protocol and pick this room. The colonel would, since it is his bedroom too. The bed is vast but we aren't heading for it. You are dragging me off to the side, to the big wardrobe. The clothes are pushed to either side and the foot-button depressed to release the catch and allow the secret door to open. We are going through to the dressing room. Only the colonel would know about this, surely? But then I *did* tell you all about it, didn't I?

We are on the couch kissing passionately now. My

mask is long forgotten and I am completely exposed. I'm trying to remember any details, any clue to let me know it's you. I can't remember how we used to kiss. I can't remember your smell. Time has washed my head clean of the memory. The feel of your large protective body is familiar though. The joy of being in your arms is the same. It was good then and it's good now, so I know it has to be you. I want to rip away your mask and see you at long last, but I'm scared I might see the colonel smiling back at me.

You are feasting on my breasts, sucking upon my nipples still hard from Tabitha's attentions. You said you would love their bigger size and this seems to be the case. The clincher is surely the way you are grasping at my bottom. You were always addicted to its softness. I couldn't get you to keep your hands off it back then, and now you are clutching each plump cheek like a long-lost friend! My bloomers are coming down so you can get your hands on my bare arse. I can feel the warmth between my legs ready to come in a deluge upon you. I would love to have you kiss and fondle me forever but my pussy is screaming to have you fill her. With my bloomers still half-off and stretched tight between my thighs I hold your cock and slowly rub the head around the entrance to my puss. I would love to have you bend me over and slam into me from the rear so you can see my bum as you fuck me. But the only way I can take you is like this, lowering myself on to you and riding you to orgasm.

My pussy lips give your cock-head a warm, wet kiss. You groan out loud, just as you had done when I held it for the first time. You can feel my wetness coating your straining glans and dripping down your shaft. I have to guide you in slowly. Centimetre by centimetre I slide down upon you, stretching myself open on your fat meat. I am hot inside but your shaft is hotter. If I wasn't so saturated I would never get you in. I feel virginal again. I let my muscles relax and slide on to you like a martyr upon a lance. Your hands are trapped between my bottom and your thighs. I stay like that awhile, getting used to your size, bathing you in my cream. Now you are lifting my bum, sliding me up your shaft and then forcing me back down, so my hot little clitty presses hard to your groin. It is sublime. Up and down I go, with you grasping my rump and lifting your head to reach my bouncing tits and suck my engorged nipples into your mouth.

Above my cloth-ears I hear the sound of the secret door opening, but my eyes stay shut until I feel her behind me. It is Tabitha. She isn't angry that we have invaded her privacy so she is either too turned on for arguments or she expected to find us here. How and why would you prearrange such a rendezvous? Unless you wanted to ensure absolute privacy with me, and her price was to be in on the act and earn your cock at last. The colonel would know to come here and she would know where to find him. But why arrange all this just to be with the man you could have every day? And why would he so specifically want me?

She is behind me, holding my tits for you to suck. My head feels like it might explode. I have you all the way inside me now and my pussy sends out another surge of juice each time it is crushed to your groin. She is spanking my arse! Fuck, the first is such a shock it goes right through me. It stings but it is good too, a dirty, lovely smarting pain that drives me into you. She is pushing at my back to get me closer to you. My bum sticks out more this way and she can give it a succession of quick slaps. She has pushed me flat to you and we are kissing again, your length inside me up to my belly. She has her hands on yours and is forcing them outwards, spreading my bum cheeks apart. I can feel her trying to lick your cock. Her nose is at my bottom. She is forcing me forward to expose more of your shaft to lick my cream from you. Then she has gripped my hips and dragged me backwards on to you again. I am going to come, any minute.

I gasp with the new tickling sensation. It's her tongue on my bumhole, the first time I have ever felt such rudeness. You are holding me open for her and she is pressing forward, trying to get inside me. I have your tongue in my mouth and hers in my bottom. I'm almost crying with bliss. She is holding my hips now. I feel a new invader at my little hole. I remember her purple dildo and let out a cry. It is already in me. I am too slippery to resist its slim girth. She holds me tight and pushes it all the way up inside me. I have never even had a finger in there before. She is pressed against my back, her nipples poking into my flesh. She humps me. She is fucking my bum! I am so full there is nothing I can do but explode. The orgasm is frighteningly massive. I hear a scream and am only vaguely aware it is from my own mouth. The juice is pouring from my pussy on to you. You hold me and keep pressing forward, to have my muscles contract against you, hugging your beautiful cock. I am still coming when she slides from me. You stay inside and manhandle me so I am over the chaise. I am no help in this, my energy and senses all gone, the bliss still bursting through my body. You pump me hard now and give me the fuck you promised me in all those dirty texts. My reservations are shot to pieces. I don't care how I look. I hope my bum is dancing the way you wanted it to. I hope I look as dirty and sexy as you claimed I would.

I hear you gasp and at last there is something I know I have a true memory of. As soon as I hear the sound I picture your face in the bathroom all those years ago. The huge wads of spunk follow but this time they are spattering my insides and not thin air. I am so happy it is you, I could die right now. You stay inside me until you are soft enough to slip out. I cannot move. I hear noises and then silence and I know you have left me to bask in my euphoria. You probably have to pay Tabitha back now for letting us have our moment at last. I don't care. She deserves to share you. Poor Michael, not getting his chance with her ... but there *must* be a next time. I lie savouring the moment, not caring who is with who. I relive your final moments, your gasp. I hear it over and over again and know it is the same as that first time in the bathroom. Only once as I replay the sound does another image jump to mind and cloud the issue. It is an image of the colonel gasping as he unloaded into his wife's mouth at that first party. I will never know for certain it was you but I will always believe that it was. I will lie here happier than ever until it is time for me to leave. Maybe you will come back and give me a sign, maybe you won't. It doesn't matter. In my heart I have had my First Love at last, and all I can do is hold out and wait for our next dirty reunion.

Club Night
Monica Belle

James wasn't sure what Lily and Rhiannon were up to, but it had to be dirty.

Every second Thursday of the month they'd come into the office as smart as paint, their hair done, in their best suits, and in stockings. James knew they wore stockings because more than once he'd got a glimpse of the soft bulge of female flesh when one or the other had accidentally revealed rather more thigh than she'd intended. They were no ordinary stockings either, but held up by suspender straps, which in turn implied sexy, expensive bras and panties beneath their outer clothes.

All day they'd be in a state of barely suppressed excitement, talking to each other in hushed, urgent tones and giggling like schoolgirls. They'd leave as early as they could, always together, and always with guilty, cautious glances towards their colleagues, as if worried they might be followed and their secret exposed. Then on the Friday they'd be all dreamy smiles, full of sultry content in a way that James had only ever seen in women after a night of really good sex.

He'd tried to find out from the start, asking half-joking questions when he happened to meet one or the other around the office or over drinks after work. Lily had laughed at him, telling him he had an overactive imagination, but Rhiannon had told him to mind his own business. That had served to confirm his suspicions, and with each passing month they'd grown stronger.

It wouldn't have been so bad if the two girls hadn't been quite so attractive. Lily was tall and slender, with jet-black hair and skin that seemed to glow with health and vitality, while everything about her – the way she walked, the way she talked, the way she held herself – spoke of a rich, enticing femininity. At a more basic level, her tight-fitting office skirts covered a pair of long sleek legs and a little round peach of a bottom, while her breasts were small and pert, with a pair of perky nipples sticking up at ten and two. Rhiannon was smaller, with an elfin figure and a riot of copper-coloured curls, a splash of freckles across a button nose, an enticingly full chest and a bouncy little bottom that wiggled as she walked.

Finally, he put his conscience aside and gave in to what he'd wanted to do from the start. Wearing glasses and an old overcoat he'd never brought to work before, he followed the girls after work. As he'd suspected, they stayed together, taking the bus to Lily's flat. James installed himself in an Indian restaurant opposite, lingering over his meal as he watched the door. His suspicions were quickly confirmed as two men arrived, both in sharp business suits, one blond, tall and handsome, the other black and taller still. A couple followed shortly after, the girl a petite blonde with an impressive chest, the man older but with an air of confidence and wealth. Last came a pretty Chinese girl wearing scarlet heels and a long coat that James suspected hid nothing but underwear, or maybe nothing but bare flesh. Lily opened the door to the newcomer, greeting her with a hug and a kiss that removed the last doubt about what was going on from James's mind. It was no friendly peck, but long, intimate and mouth to mouth, the sort of kiss that suggested all sorts of intriguing possibilities.

A few minutes later Rhiannon appeared at the window to pull the curtains closed. James was left seething with frustration and erotic fantasies as he imagined what might be going on. At the very least the girls had some sort of swinging club, and with four girls but only three men it wasn't just going to be a night of partner swapping. The way Lily had greeted the Chinese girl suggested a strong possibility that the girls would be playing together, perhaps putting on a show for the men. It was all too easy to picture, in a thousand exciting permutations: the Chinese girl kneeling to lick Lily's sex, Rhiannon and the little blonde naked in a sixty-nine as they brought each other to ecstasy, all four girls together on the floor in the nude, stroking and kissing and licking at each other's breasts and bottoms and cunts.

James left the restaurant with a straining erection so urgently in need of attention that he was forced to bring himself off in a public lavatory, something he'd never done before. Even afterwards, as he made his way home full of embarrassment for what he'd done, he couldn't keep the vivid images of what the girls might have been doing out of his mind. A four-pack of beer only made things worse and his head was still spinning with jealousy and lust when he finally managed to find sleep shortly before dawn, by which time he'd masturbated until his cock was sore.

From that moment on joining the girls at their games became the most important thing in his life. He did his best to get close to them, forcing himself to be patient and not to make himself appear desperate, until at last he felt that the time was right. With a few days to go before the next Thursday party, he managed to arrange a quiet moment with the two of them in a local bar, sharing a bottle of wine before putting the question he so desperately needed to ask.

'Hey, so the party this Thursday. How about I get an invite?'

Lily made to laugh his question off, as she always did, but Rhiannon gave him a proper answer.

'I don't think it would really be your thing.'

James gave his most winning smile. 'Hey, come on, you know me! We get on, don't we? I've more or less guessed what happens, just from the way you are on Friday mornings. You know I can keep a secret too.'

This time it was Lily who answered. 'It's not like that. We don't mind you, but you need to be pretty open minded.'

'This is me we're talking about! I invented open minded.'

Lily and Rhiannon shared a look, then rose as one to walk quickly to the Ladies as James's eyes followed their legs. He knew they'd be talking about him, deciding his fate, and he was praying that all his efforts to ingratiate himself with them while not losing his innate masculinity would bear fruit. They'd certainly been friendly, and if there was one thing he was confident in it was his looks, with his lean, muscular body and intense, thoughtful eyes.

Sure enough, when the girls returned both smiling, Lily amused and a little excited, Rhiannon full of mischief.

Lily spoke. 'OK, you can come, but what goes on at

the Club stays at the Club, and you have to play by the rules.'

James was fighting to hide his emotions as he replied. 'You got it. Anything you say.'

Rhiannon was insistent, and there was a touch of colour in her cheeks. 'Swear you won't tell anybody else, James.'

'I swear. You know you can trust me.'

Lily laughed. 'Of course we can trust you, especially after you've played a couple of times.'

***

James spent the next few days on a natural high that nothing could break. He now shared the secret, and each time he saw Lily or Rhiannon they would favour him with a knowing smile or a teasing word. By Thursday he was fired up to the point of finding it hard to concentrate on anything but the prospect of what might happen that evening, and he was ready to leave long before Lily came to collect him from his desk.

He was singing inside as the three of them took the short bus journey to her flat, and as he helped to arrange the square, comfortably decorated living room in which the party was to take place. Other people began to arrive, first the couple, Alan and Trisha, then the two men, Nathan and Lloyd, lastly the Chinese girl, Xiang. All were well dressed and well groomed, smart without being overtly sexual or slutty, and James found it impossible to decide which of the four girls was the most attractive. Lily and Rhiannon were as lovely as ever, but there was a delicious softness to Trisha that suggested a vulnerable, giving nature, while Xiang not only looked exquisitely formed beneath her short dress of vivid blue silk but also had an intriguingly wanton touch to her manner.

Lily played her part as hostess, making sure everybody had drinks, introducing James to each person as they arrived, lighting candles and shutting the curtains to leave the room bathed in soft yellow light. She'd also brought out several bowls from the kitchen, some with nuts, others with olives, one full to the top with condoms, which could mean only one thing – she and the other girls were expecting to be fucked.

With everything ready she came to sit down next to him, her perfume making his head swim and the casual touch of her hand to his knee sending a jolt of pleasure to his cock. She was holding a small velvet bag, a blue notepad and several pens, which she began to dish out as she spoke to James.

'We always play a game, because it's more fun that way. Tonight's is an old favourite. Write down two of your favourite fantasies, stuff we can do between us, fold the piece of paper and put it in the bag. We take turns to draw and, whatever you get, you have to do. You can play it safe, or you can be daring, or cruel. So let's say you've always wanted me to get it on with Rhiannon. You'd write down "oral sex with Rhiannon", and, if I pick it, I have to do it.'

James nodded, his mouth too dry to speak, and picked up two of the little pieces of paper. For a moment he wondered how far he could go, and how personal he could get, but there was no mistaking the girls' arousal, or the implications of the condoms and of what Lily had said. Leaning back, he wrote 'oral sex with Rhiannon', then 'has to fuck with James'. After carefully folding each piece of paper, he placed them in the bag. The others did the same, each passing the bag around until all of them had put in their two pieces of paper, finishing with Rhiannon. She shook the bag, her eyes alight with excitement as she cast a glance around the room.

'Who's first? James, maybe, as he's new.'

A sudden tightening of his stomach and James realised he wasn't ready to play yet, not until he'd watched some of the others. He made what he hoped would look like a gallant gesture. 'Ladies first.'

Nobody objected and Rhiannon pushed her hand into the bag, only for her happy grin to turn to shock as she read what was on the paper. 'Lily, you bitch!'

Lily laughed. 'Got you! I knew I would in the end. Which one is it?'

'The spanking. You're such a little pervert, Lily Sands!'

She was trying to make a joke of it, and she'd already got to her feet, but her voice sounded genuinely sulky, filling James with an odd mixture of excitement and guilt.

Lily clearly had no doubts whatsoever, sitting forward on the sofa to make a lap as Rhiannon approached and addressing her friend and victim in a voice full of sadistic delight. 'Come on, darling, the whole nine yards, over my knee, skirt up and panties pulled down.'

Rhiannon made a face but did as she was told, draping herself across Lily's lap with her bottom raised. She looked genuinely sorry for herself, with her pretty face set in a look of bitter consternation that grew quickly stronger as her office skirt was tucked up and the smart black panties beneath turned down to expose her bottom. Her head was dangling down by James's legs and she'd been tipped up to make her bottom the highest part of her body, leaving her firm, fleshy cheeks just far enough open for him to make out the pale dimple of her anus. It was impossible not to enjoy the view, and Lily evidently felt the same way, her happy smile growing broader still as she began to stroke her friend's bottom.

Rhiannon had hung her head, apparently resigned to her ignominious bare-bottom spanking, but spoke up as Lily began to tease between her cheeks. 'That tickles! You said a spanking, Lily, nothing about molesting me!'

Lily was unfazed. 'Having your bottom touched is all

part of the punishment, darling, but, seeing as you're so keen to get on with the spanking, here we go.'

She'd begun to spank even before she'd finished speaking, applying regular swats to Rhiannon's naked bottom, hard enough to make the redhead kick and squeal in mingled pain and indignation. James could only stare, at once horrified and fascinated, deeply sorry for Rhiannon even as his cock began to grow in his pants. None of the others seemed to have any reservations at all, all three men with their gazes fixed on Rhiannon's bare, jiggling bottom and the rear view of her cunt, while Trisha was giggling openly and Xiang's mouth had curled up into a cruel smile. Rhiannon made no effort to hide her emotion, squealing and gasping her way through the spanking, with her legs kicking wide to show off her rear view, while her bottom had been turned a rosy pink and tears had begun to trickle from her eyes before Lily finally stopped.

'There we are, one spanked bottom. I have wanted to do that for ages, Rhiannon.'

Rhiannon got up, blowing out her breath as she reached back to rub and squeeze at her well-smacked rear cheeks. As she kneaded her flesh she was showing off her anus and the mouth of her cunt, which James couldn't help but notice was wet with juice, although that didn't seem to make her any less resentful as she answered her friend. 'Just you wait, Lily. I'll get you back.'

'Maybe, if you're lucky. Meanwhile, don't forget, what's bare stays bare, so you can leave your panties down and your skirt right where it is.'

Rhiannon didn't answer, but made no move to adjust herself, sitting her bare bottom down on her chair and blowing out her breath before picking up the bag once more. 'Your turn, James.'

James was grinning as Rhiannon held out the bag to him, imagining all the delicious possibilities as he pulled out a piece of paper and unfolded it, only to laugh as he saw what was written. 'Oops! This is one for a girl – "Suck the guy with the biggest cock." Hang on.'

He'd reached out to take another piece of paper, but Rhiannon had withdrawn the bag, her eyes glittering mischief as she spoke. 'Uh, uh, that's not the way it works. You have to do whatever you get.'

'But I'm not gay!'

There was more than a touch of scorn in Rhiannon's voice as she answered him. 'So? I'm not a lesbian, but I just let Lily spank me. You enjoyed that, didn't you?'

'Yeah, but you're girls.'

'Oh, right, so it's OK for girls to do dirty things to each other so men can get their kicks, but not OK for girls to want to see men do it?'

Now the scorn in her voice was so rich that James found himself wilting. There was no denying the logic of her argument, except that it went against everything he'd always accepted as normal. He turned to the other men. 'Yeah, but, come on, guys, whoever it would be, you don't want me sucking your cock, do you? You want one of the girls.'

Lloyd answered him. 'Those are the rules, James. What you get, you do. That's half the thrill, and, anyway, I bet your mouth's just as warm and wet as any of the girls', so, yeah, you can suck me.'

James swallowed, realising that it was probably the tall, solidly built black man he was expected to go down on. It was an appalling thought, and made far worse because it would be in front of an audience, including Lily and Rhiannon.

'And what if I just refuse to do it?'

Rhiannon shrugged. 'Easy. You don't get invited next time. I said he couldn't take his medicine, Lily.'

'Maybe you were right. Come on, James. You said you could handle it.'

James could feel the mood in the room turning against him and made a last desperate bid to escape his humiliation. 'What if I've got the biggest cock?'

Lloyd shook his head. 'I don't think so.'

As he spoke he'd put his hand to his fly, and now pulled it down and burrowed in to pull out his cock and balls. Like everybody else, he'd been turned on by watching Rhiannon's spanking and he was already half-hard, his cock a great fat club of dark-brown man meat with a deep-pink head the size of a golf ball poking out from a heavy foreskin. James could only stare in horror as the black man went on. 'If you're bigger than me, I'll suck you.'

James tried to reply but only managed to produce an odd gurgling noise as he stared at the enormous cock now lying in Lloyd's hand. He'd always been proud of the size of his cock, but he simply wasn't in the same league.

Trisha gave a gentle sigh. 'You're beautiful, Lloyd. Who wouldn't want to suck you?'

James found his voice. 'You're welcome, Trisha.'

She gave him a bright, easy smile. 'No, no, he's for you, this time. You'll like it, once you get down to it, believe me.'

James shook his head, but she'd stood up and now walked over to him, first to stroke his hair and then to take him by the hand as she went on. 'Come on, James. I know it's difficult, and maybe it's even your first time, but you'll love it, you really will. You're a giving person, James, I know you are, and there's nothing more giving than to take a man in your mouth.'

Rhiannon added her voice. 'She's right, James. And besides, I'll respect you for it, and who knows, maybe you'll get me later?'

Nathan put in, 'We've all done it, mate.'

Then Lily, her voice thick with arousal, whispered, 'I

want to see you do it, James. I want to see you suck Lloyd's cock.'

James was still trying to think of a way out, but he'd allowed Trisha to help him to his feet and all the others seemed to be talking at once, every single one in favour of him going down on the monstrous black cock being offered to his mouth.

'Go on. You'll love it, and I so want to watch.'

'You can have me if you do it, game or no game.'

'You just need to get over yourself, James.'

'Just open your mouth and let it in.'

'That's right, down on your knees, you cocksucking little bitch.'

Xiang had spoken last, and her sharp, high voice nearly broke the spell that had been building in James's head, but it was too late. He was already kneeling in front of Lloyd, kneeling to give head just like any of the girls who'd sucked him across the years, his mouth already half-open, the thick, masculine smell of Lloyd's cock strong in his senses. One last time he tried to pull away, only for the black man's hand to close gently but firmly in his hair. As his head was pulled down he found his jaw coming wide despite himself. His lips touched the meaty head and at the realisation that he'd kissed another man's cock the last of his resistance broke. His jaw came wider still, to allow Lloyd to feed in his monstrous cock, and, after a moment of just holding the horrible, irresistible thing in his mouth, James had begun to suck. Lloyd gave a deep sigh and relaxed back into his chair, but kept a firm grip in James's hair, and on his cock, pulling gently up and down on the shaft.

James had shut his eyes, unable to cope with the sight of Lloyd masturbating into his mouth, yet there was no longer any need for the hand in his hair. From the moment he'd taken Lloyd's cock into his mouth he'd got the urge to suck, and he was doing it, for all his self-disgust and humiliation, moving his lips back and forth on the thick shaft and using his tongue to lick at the meaty foreskin, just the way he liked it himself. Not only that, but a sense of weakness had begun to creep up on him, a feeling that he was where he belonged, on his knees with a cock in his mouth, if only because Lloyd was so big and so blatantly virile. The others obviously agreed, the girls sighing and giggling, the men talking in low voices, relieved that it wasn't them doing the cock-sucking, but with envy too.

At last Lloyd spoke up. 'Yeah, he likes it. I knew he would. Come on, boy, play with my balls.'

James had obeyed before he could stop himself, reaching up to cup Lloyd's heavy sack in his hand, stroking the wrinkled skin and rolling the fat balls within over his fingers. Lloyd immediately lifted himself in the chair, to push down his trousers and the boxer shorts beneath, exposing himself fully as James continued to suck and the others to watch in delight. Slowly, James let his eyes come open, still horrified by what he was doing, but far more horrified by the truth of what Lloyd had said. For all the humiliation raging in his head, for all the pathetic sense of emasculation building within him, he was enjoying his suck.

His efforts seemed to be working too. Lloyd had begun to swell, his great club of a cock growing fatter and firmer in James's mouth, a disgusting sensation that only made him want to suck harder. He tried to take Lloyd deep, gripping the thick cock shaft and rolling back the foreskin to push the bloated helmet into his throat, only to find himself gagging. Lloyd gave a contented sigh and pushed himself up, forcing James to do it again, and at the feel of the fat cock-head pressing into his throat something inside him snapped.

He began to suck hard, squeezing the fat black balls and wanking Lloyd's now turgid shaft into his mouth, kissing and sucking at the meaty head, licking under the now taut foreskin, before once more taking as much cock as he could get down his throat, until he began to gag. Xiang laughed to see him so urgent, a high-pitched giggle of pure glee, but James no longer cared. He was busy giving a blow job and that was all that mattered.

Lloyd was fully erect, his cock a great tower of hard black meat with the heavy balls hanging beneath. Still James sucked, ignoring the voice in the back of his head that was trying to tell him he'd done his task and he was now just being a dirty cock-sucking little slut. It was what he wanted to be, and most of all he wanted to suffer the final humiliation and make his man come in his mouth, then swallow the spunk, only for Lloyd to suddenly grab him by the hair again and pull him back.

'Cool down, yeah? I don't want to lose it in your mouth.'

Lily chimed in. 'We've got the whole evening, James.'

James rocked back on his heels, furiously embarrassed at his behaviour and not least because his own cock was rock hard in his pants. Yet nobody seemed to mind, just the opposite, and Rhiannon thanked him for the show as she passed Lloyd the bag.

'That was good to see. You're next then, Lloyd.'

Lloyd nodded and plunged his hand into the bag, to pull out a piece of paper, unfold it and read out what had been written.

Has to fuck with James.

Sauce for the Gander
Terri Pray

Pippa glanced at the clock and then forced herself to look away. Maybe this hadn't been such a good idea after all? It wasn't the type of thing she normally did but it had made sense when they'd first discussed it. She reached for her glass of wine, took a quick sip and set it back down on the table.

How long had she been waiting for Richard to show up anyway?

She resisted the urge to look at the clock again. It couldn't have been more than thirty seconds since the last time she'd checked.

'Pippa?'

She looked up at the sound of the voice and smiled. 'Hello, Richard.'

The tall man with soft, curly light-brown hair smiled back at her and settled into the chair opposite at the small table Pippa had claimed. 'I wasn't sure you'd be here.'

'I almost didn't go through with it. The way he looked at me …'

'Charles? I understand; Brenda was the same way this morning.' He shook his head. 'Funny, don't you think? I mean, they've been carrying on for over two years but they have a problem with us meeting up like this.'

Pippa's throat tightened. 'No, I don't think they do really. I guess they thought we wouldn't go through with it, that's all.'

Richard reached across the table and took hold of her hand, gently rubbing his thumb over the back of her knuckles. 'Pippa, this isn't about revenge for me. You know that, don't you?'

'They still love us, don't they?'

'Yes, I've no doubt of that. I don't understand it though.' Richard moved his hand away from hers and reached out to cup her chin, lifting her gaze to meet his. 'You're a beautiful, sensual woman, Pippa. I've always known that. Always seen that in you. Don't hide it from me, not tonight at least. There's something untamed within you but I don't think you've ever had the chance to let it out. All I'm asking you is that you let the walls down tonight, don't lock me out, or keep yourself locked away.'

A soft flush crept across her cheeks. 'I'll try not to.'

Were they doing the right thing? She leaned into his touch, closing her eyes for a moment as the conversation with Charles replayed in the back of her mind.

'*Don't knock what you haven't tried, love. This has kept our marriage alive in more ways than I can count.*'

'So tell me why you want this, Pippa.' He dropped his hand away from her chin. 'Do you want me?'

'Yes, heaven help me, I do.' She looked away from him, trying to take a few moments to bring her thoughts back into order.

'Why?'

She took a deep breath and met his gaze. 'I've always been curious about what it would be like to be with you.'

'Why is that?'

'You're very different to Charles. He's so – so formal, correct, if you will. Business suits, short perfect hair, well-polished shoes and everything in its place. You work with your hands, your hair is long, always looks like it needs combing even if you've just tidied it up.' She flushed and continued. 'I don't mean anything bad by that. Just – well – you're very unconventional compared to Charles.'

'You're afraid you've offended me?' He smiled and shook his head. 'Well, you haven't. Not in the slightest. I am who I am. I work with machines and have my arms elbow-deep in grease, oil and engine parts most days.

There's grease under my fingers even after I've showered, so I'm very unlike Charles and I think this is the first time I've worn a shirt in years.'

'It's not just that. I like the way you look at me.'

'How is that?'

She reached out and picked up the wineglass, cupping it between her fingers. 'As if you're undressing me, slowly. You never acted on it, but I could see it in your gaze.'

'You're an interesting woman, Pippa.' He leaned back in his chair. 'I've wanted to undress you since the day Charles first introduced us. But you were with Charles and I didn't want to risk the friendship I had – still have – with Charles.'

That was the odd thing. The news of the affair hadn't ended their friendships. Nor had it destroyed either marriage. Instead, it had opened up the door to this situation. 'And Brenda?'

'She's fairly sure she can handle this if it works out. Charles?'

'He's open to the idea.'

'Brenda asked me why; all I could think of was that old saying.' He smiled when she gave him a questioning look. 'What's sauce for the goose is sauce for the gander.'

'Ouch.' She winced.

'No, not really. She said she understood that. She just wasn't sure if you were the right one for me or vice versa.'

Pippa leaned back in her chair and took a swallow from the wineglass. More than she'd originally planned on drinking. 'I should be hurt by that, but I'm not. Brenda is a good person but she's a little blind when it comes to people who aren't like – like her.'

'A little blind – I think that's the nicest way anyone has described her.' Richard waved over a waiter and ordered a drink. When the waiter had gone Richard sighed. 'I love my wife; I don't think that will ever change, but she can be a very challenging individual to live with.'

'I'm still in love with Charles,' Pippa admitted. 'Even after everything that's come to light. I mean, you'd think I'd want him out of my life for cheating on me, but I don't. Is that wrong?'

'No, I don't think so. I feel the same way about Brenda.' He paused as the waiter set a drink in front of him, continuing only when the waiter had left. 'So, it boils down to this: do you want to back out, or shall we see where our desires will take us?' His voice was a soft, deep and very sensual purr.

Pippa met his warm gaze and smiled. His dark eyes offered a chance of seduction, delicious slow lovemaking that she couldn't turn away from. If she said no there'd be no second chance at this and she found that she wasn't ready to turn her back on that. 'Yes, I want to do this.'

'Good.' He took a swig from his glass. 'Shall we? Or did you want to have something to eat first?'

Pippa finished off her drink and set the glass down on the table. 'I've already checked in.' She'd done that when she first arrived and her overnight case was already in the room.

'Good. I wasn't sure if you had or not and didn't want to try to book into the room until we'd spoken.' He waved the waiter over and paid the bill. Once that was done he stood up and waited for Pippa to do the same.

She glanced around. Did anyone here know what they were about to do? Could they see she was about to cheat on her husband? Except, was it cheating if everyone knew and had agreed to it? She followed Richard out of the quiet hotel bar without a word.

The hair on the back of her neck rose and she fought the urge to turn and leave the hotel. Then she felt it, his arm slipping around her waist as he pulled her in close to shelter her within the circle of his embrace.

Her anxiety slipped away and she sighed in relief. Safe and something more. His touch sparked a heat that crept across her breasts, pebbling both of her nipples. Her breath hitched and she forced herself to focus on walking with him through the lobby to the lift.

'What's our room number?'

'One-Three-Seven.' She didn't even have to look at the key folder to know that. Odd, she missed real room keys right now. A real key, instead of a plastic card, would have added to the growing feeling of delicious wickedness that even now seeped through her being and down between her thighs.

'Not far up then. Good, I don't think I want to wait much longer, Pippa.' He moved his hand down from her waist and slipped it behind her, cupping her buttock through her skirt once they'd stepped into the lift and the doors had shut.

Her eyes closed and she leaned back into his touch. God, this wasn't what she'd expected. She turned, wrapping her arms about his neck and lifting up on to her toes, closing the distance between their lips.

'Hmm, something you wanted, Pippa?' A teasing smile played across his lips.

'You,' she admitted and tried to kiss him.

Richard held back, smiling as he shook his head. 'Not here.' He jerked his head towards the upper left-hand corner of the lift where a small camera was attached to the wall. 'We don't want to give them a show, do we?'

Before Pippa had a chance to answer, the lift stopped and the doors opened. Would it really have been so bad to be watched? She didn't have an answer for him this time.

A moment later she swiped the card through the lock and smiled as the door clicked open. If she had any last doubts now was the time to voice them. Except, no matter how closely she examined her motives or her attraction to Richard, she couldn't find a single objection. This was the right thing to do for her, for him, for both of them. This wasn't about revenge; neither of them really felt any drive to get their own back on their spouses. No, this was about desires that had been kept under control for far too many years now.

Desires they would finally have the chance to explore.

The door closed behind them and she smiled up at him. 'No cameras here, Richard.'

'No, so what shall we do about that?' He pressed one hand against the door on either side of her head.

She reached up, wrapping her arms about his neck as she lifted on to her toes, bringing her lips close to his. 'How about this?' She brushed her lips softly against his.

'A good start.' He smiled against her lips. 'But I was thinking of something more like this.' He leaned in close, pinning Pippa against the door. He growled against her lips, his tongue parting hers in a firm, full thrust.

She groaned, her eyes closing as she surrendered beneath his kiss, her arms tightening about his neck. His tongue probed, tasted and tested the soft walls of her mouth. The sensual intruder stroked her tongue, challenging her to respond but she held back, uncertain if it would be the right thing to do. She wasn't this forward; even the brush kiss had been more than she would normally do. Yet with him it felt right. There were no expectations with Richard.

He pulled back from the kiss. 'Just let the walls down, Pippa. Trust me. I'm not going to judge you no matter what you do.'

104

Pippa opened her eyes and met his gaze, searching for some sign that he wasn't telling the truth. He'd never lied to her, not that she'd been aware of, so why would he start now?

He wouldn't.

She stepped away from the door and fully into his embrace, her lips finding and seeking his neck. She nibbled, kissing, teasing with her teeth, lips and tongue, forging a path from his jaw down to his collar. He groaned beneath the sensual passage of her teeth.

'Oh, God, yes.' He tipped his head back, baring his throat to her touch. 'That's good,' he growled.

Pippa smiled at his words, urged on by them as she reached between his thighs, cupping his hardening cock through the cloth. She wasn't like this normally, but timid and careful. Not this bold touch that she now enjoyed.

'That's it.' His cock twitched under her caress.

Powerful, that's how she felt right now, powerful and eager to explore the pleasures he now offered her. All she had to do was let her imagination take control and who knew where it would lead?

'You're wearing too much, Richard.'

'Then do something about it.' He took a step away from her.

She frowned, annoyed at the distance he'd suddenly put between them. 'Why did you move?'

'Perhaps I want you to work for what you want, Pippa.' He grinned and took another step towards the bed. 'Take what you want, Pippa. Let that hidden part of you escape even if it only happens this once.'

Was he serious?

There was only one way to find out.

Pippa kicked off her shoes and stalked towards him. 'If I catch you, then what?'

'You get to do whatever you want with me, until I change my mind and get my own back.' He grinned.

'Sounds good to me.' She took a step towards him again, trying to judge which way he would move.

Richard darted to the left, laughing as he did so. 'Have to be faster than that, Pippa!'

'Oh, I intend to be!' Her heart pounded, nipples hard against the cups of her bra as she dashed after him. What was she going to do when she got close to him?

'Is that all you've got?' He taunted her when she missed him by a finger-length. 'You're faster than that, I know you are.'

She half-dived across the bed, grasping him by the arm of his shirt. 'Mine!'

He laughed and didn't try to break free. 'Well, you caught me but now what are you going to do with me?'

She edged off the bed, still holding him by the sleeve and glanced at the bed. Did she want him there or ...?

No, he was still wearing too much. 'Don't move.'

She reached for the buttons on his shirt, smiling as he did what she'd told him to do. 'Don't move at all.'

'Your wish is my command.' He smiled as she undid the first button. 'Hmm, I think I could get used to this. A beautiful woman slowly undressing me isn't something that happens every day.'

She bit back the temptation to ask questions that she wasn't sure she even wanted the answer to. Instead, she undid one button at a time, parting the fabric of the shirt until she tugged the tails out of his trousers. Without a word she slid her fingers under the shoulders of his shirt and eased it down his back. When it caught, briefly, at his wrists, she tugged it off and tossed it to the floor.

A soft mat of brown hair covered his chest and formed a V down to his navel. So unlike the smooth, hairless chest her husband sported that it almost caught her off guard. Had she seen him without a shirt or T-shirt before?

Pippa traced her fingers through the soft curls, tugging lightly on them.

'Like what you see?'

'Yes.' She leaned in, resting her cheek against his chest. 'I do.' She reached for his belt and slipped it out of the loops, before tossing it on the floor along with the shirt. 'Kick your shoes off.'

He did.

'And step out of your trousers.' She moved back from him, giving him the room to strip.

Richard took off his trousers and hooked his thumbs into the sides of his underpants, his cock straining against the material. 'And these?'

'Take them off. Slowly.' She licked her lips as she watched him, the sense of power, control, buzzing through her blood. 'Very slowly.' Her heart raced, and she fought the urge to reach out to him, to touch him again. The feel of his hair, the texture, the way it played off between his chest and her touch, had left her hands tingling. What would the rest of him feel like?

Richard let his underpants drop, freeing his thick long cock and she felt her breath hitch. His balls, heavy and large, hung between his thighs and she moved before she realised it, cupping them in her hands.

'Fuck,' he sighed.

She rolled them gently between her fingers, watching as his cock bobbed, a small glistening bead of pre-come forming on the head. She wanted to taste it, taste him, but she wasn't the type to drop on her knees and suck a man off. Charles always grabbed her by the hair and that panicked her. But this was different, right? He'd said she was in control. Well, perhaps she should use that.

'Put your hands behind your head and don't move them.'

'Hmm, sounds fun.' He grinned and lifted his hands, locking them behind his head. 'What do you have planned?'

'Just wait and see.' She lowered herself slowly to her knees in front of him.

He groaned, his cock twitching in front of her lips. 'God, you don't know how often I've thought of you kneeling in front of me like this.'

'Don't move. I mean it, you move and I stop.' She looked up at him, holding his balls in her hand and squeezing them gently. 'I'm in charge here, or I walk out of the door.'

'Agreed.' He lifted on to his toes until she eased the pressure on his balls. 'I'm all yours, my lady.'

'My lady. I could get to like that.' She closed her lips around the head of his cock, teasing it with the tip of her tongue. She kept one hand between his thighs, holding his balls, the other wrapped around the base of his cock, squeezing and releasing it in time to the probing of her testing tongue.

His cock throbbed in her hand and the strength of his taste increased, a new bead forming on the head which she quickly cleaned with a swipe of her tongue. She was in control here. She could take as much or as little of his cock in her mouth as she wished to and there was nothing he could do to change that.

She closed her lips fully around the head of his cock and slowly eased down the length of it, licking and sucking. He groaned, arching his hips, though he made no move to reach for her head. It wasn't easy to take him, and she didn't try to take his entire length, not this time, but she eased her lips slowly down his cock.

Moist heat dampened her panties and she squirmed,

more aroused by the control she now had over Richard than the feel of his cock in her mouth. She scraped her teeth very gently back over the length of his cock until she reached the head and then looked up at him through the veil of her hair.

'Fuck!' he growled, struggling to maintain position.

'That's what I have in mind.' She moved to her feet, letting go of his cock and balls. 'On the bed, on your back, and grip the headboard.'

He moved to the bed without a word of complaint and Pippa focused on shedding her clothing. Her dress, panties and bra all joined her shoes on the floor but after a short pause she kept her hold-up stockings on. Only then did she walk to the bed and the waiting Richard.

'Don't move and don't let go of the headboard.'

'Pippa, God – you're beautiful. You don't know how much I want to touch you. How I've longed for this or something like this.' His breathing was ragged as he watched every move she made.

'Just remember, you move and I'll dress and then leave. I want control of what happens between us.' Why though? This wasn't normal for her; Pippa knew that, just as she knew this was something she couldn't give up. Not this time.

Richard nodded, his gaze never leaving Pippa's nearly nude form.

Her pussy clenched as her own gaze moved to Richard's

thick throbbing cock. What would it be like to feel that buried deep within her?

There was only one way to find out.

Pippa climbed on to the bed and straddled Richard, her knees planted on either side of him as she found her balance, her silken, heated core centred over his cock. Then it hit her. If he was to stay still with his hands firmly gripping the headboard, that meant she would have to take hold of his cock to ease it within her body. She flushed at the thought and then shook it off. She had already pushed herself further than she thought possible so what was one step more?

She reached down and carefully gripped his cock with her left hand. It twitched in her grasp, the head coated with a large bead of glistening pre-come. Slowly, his cock still in her hand, she lowered her hips until the head of his cock nestled between her nether lips.

Richard groaned, arching his hips off the bed.

'Careful, you're coming very close to breaking the agreement.'

He gave a sheepish smile and pressed his hips back against the bed.

The head of his cock entered her and she hissed, her walls tightening on it. She closed her eyes, struggling for self-control, knowing that, if she lost it, she'd push down, fully, on his cock in one thrust. It would all be over too quickly if she did that.

Inch by inch she lowered herself on to his cock, letting it fill her and stretch her walls until she buried him to the hilt within her slick heat. She groaned, resting her hands on his abdomen, not moving for several long minutes, letting her body become used to the feel of him deep within her body. Then she began to move.

She danced on him, moving her hips, circling them first to the left, then to the right, tipping her hips at the high point on each circle. Once she had her balance she lifted her hands from his body and moved them to her own breasts, cupping them as she danced. Her thighs strained, her inner walls clenching and releasing in time to the sensual circling of her hips.

Richard's eyes widened and his knuckles went white as he gripped the headboard. He groaned, his head tipping back as he struggled to stay still under her.

Pippa moved one hand down between her thighs, pinching her left nipple with the other hand. Then her fingers began a rapid swirling over her slick, hard clit.

Her hips moved faster with each passing moment, her breath ragged, nipples hard as she pleasured herself on him. Using him. Taking him. Sweat beaded across her breasts and still she moved, circling her hips, twisting down on him, taking herself higher, until he groaned, his head jerking up, his gaze fixed on her. 'I can't hold on!'

'You can and you will. For me!' Pippa commanded, straining to speak through the pleasure that even now threatened to take control of her body. 'Just a little longer, Richard.'

'Trying to – God, I'm trying to.'

She no longer heard him. All she knew was the sound of her blood beating a rapid path through her body. A path that pulsed in her nipples and clit and along the inner walls of her pussy. She groaned, dancing, pressing down on him and let her body command her actions instead of her mind.

Pressure pushed down into the pit of her being. Hunger she couldn't deny set the pace of her hips. With each passing moment it grew, becoming something more than it had been a heartbeat before. She sobbed, tipping her head back, crying out to him. 'Come for me!

'Yes!' He cried out, his hands still locked in a death grip on the headboard. His hips arched, lifting from the bed, his muscles taut and tendons straining as his cock pulsed within her.

Her cry joined with his. Her thighs still clenched around him as she pressed down one last time, sobbing as the pressure rocked through her, threatening to strip her of her sanity. For one brief moment neither of them moved, locked in an arch of pleasure and then she collapsed.

How long she lay, sprawled across his chest, Pippa didn't know. Her mind crawled back through the fog and she swatted at the curl of hair that insisted on tickling the end of her nose. Only then did she realise that there was an arm curled protectively around her shoulders and the full memory of what they had shared came back to her.

'Hello, my lady.' Richard spoke softly when Pippa raised her head to look at him. 'Thank you.'

'I don't understand.' Speaking wasn't easy. Her throat was sore and she blushed remembering how she'd all but screamed in pleasure.

'For letting the walls down.'

Pippa smiled and nuzzled against his chest. 'You're welcome.'

'This isn't going to be a one-off thing between us, is it, Pippa.' A statement, not a question.

'No, it's not.' She smiled and closed her eyes. There would be other evenings or perhaps afternoons that they would share. Lots of them if she had her way. After all, Richard was right. What was sauce for the goose was most certainly sauce for her gander ...

Risk Reduction
Madeline Moore

Nikki wanted sex. All night long she'd dreamed of sex with strangers and she'd awakened with the female equivalent of a hard-on. Unfortunately, since she'd slept through the alarm, there'd been no time to slip her hand between her thighs and stroke her buzzing clit to climax.

Work had been busy, at least. And the 'sublimate your sexual energy' approach she'd been taught by Dr McConnelly had worked. She'd rocked her job. But busy meant lunch at her desk and coffee on the run. No time to duck into a cubicle in the ladies' room and soothe her snatch with some three-finger thrusts and a thumb diddle, never mind indulge in a little daydreaming about lunching *under* the gorgeous new CEO's desk, he of the six-pack abs and guns that bulged when he shot his cuffs.

Dr McConnelly allowed her fantasy as a form of risk reduction. He and Nikki were almost but not entirely sure that, disinhibited though she may be, she'd learned her lesson at her previous job. It still made her blush and cringe and, admittedly, laugh to think about it.

Nikki hadn't been on the sales team for the San Francisco-based firm very long when the holiday season hit. What a party her company had provided! Being very young (this had been a few years ago), she'd drunk way too much champagne and decided to blow the boss.

He was cute and married so she'd likely have gotten away with the fast and dirty cocksucking she'd performed in the men's room. But they'd been caught by a co-worker so nothing would do but that she blew him, too. And another, and another, and soon guys were telling other guys, 'Nikki's giving holiday blow jobs in the men's room!' It'd been glorious, really: down on her knees, not caring about the ladders in her stockings or the stains on her crimson satin party dress; the smell of sex and sweat and cologne surrounding her; all those hard cocks coming at her; cream running down her chin; the groans of the one coming in her mouth mingled with the cheers and moans of those already spent or waiting their turn. Mm.

But she'd been terminated before the hangover had worn off. Never again, Nikki. Never again would she drink so much or sink to her knees for even one workmate, let alone a dozen or more. She'd moved from the west coast to the east and started using her middle name as her first. And she'd gone into therapy with the marvellous, patient, brilliant and adorably Irish Dr McConnelly.

Nikki left work early, as she had one Friday a month for the three years she'd been with her present firm, to meet with him. They were winding down their sessions. He was taking early retirement and she'd learned plenty about boundaries, which was what he'd decided she needed after she told him her version of a Christmas story.

Boundaries. First, she'd learned what they were. Then she'd established some of her own. Then she'd learned to respect the boundaries of others. Nikki had come a long way in therapy, but she wasn't looking forward to the day when she was released by Dr McConnelly and unleashed, solo, upon the world.

Nikki rose from the metro at the proper station and tip-tapped along the sidewalk in her high heels. She wore heels the way other women wore crocs. Her straight-cut black hair just brushed the collar of her stylish charcoal jacket. The matching short skirt showed off mile-long legs that were sheathed in dark stockings and then those killer black leather heels. If she attracted a few glances from the men and returned them with appreciative glances of her own, that was OK, right?

Maybe she'd talk to Dr McConnelly about it.

What she really wanted to do was kiss Dr McConnelly. They'd worked through her 'transference' period where she'd been desperately in love with him and terrified he'd find out. It'd been embarrassing, stupid even, but it was long over. He'd promised that someday she'd come to regard him with indifference but that day hadn't arrived and now that he was taking early retirement it likely wouldn't. Nikki no longer fantasised endlessly about fucking Dr McConnelly, but she still had to battle a desire to flash him while crossing her legs, or brush her breasts against him when he took her coat, or just touch his hand as he wrote out their next appointment in his looping script.

'How are you?' Dr McConnelly's pale-blue eyes were focused on her, his position in the leather wingback chair relaxed but alert. God, he was good at his job.

'The truth is I've been sexually needy all day.'

He blushed, as he always did when they discussed sex. She'd seen him blush many times over the years. They both ignored it now. 'Have you contacted your "Friends"?'

'I've been texting all day. No luck. But it's Friday. Even for Friends With Benefits it's a little late.'

'Masturbation?'

'There wasn't time this morning. I suppose that'll have to do, tonight, but as you know after a certain point it just makes me blue. And I've reached that point.'

'Hmmm. Shall we go over the list of things you *aren't* going to do?'

Nikki ticked off the items on her fingers as she recited them out loud. 'I'm not going to approach any of my girlfriends' husbands, even though Janet's away for the weekend and her husband Graham clearly lusts after me.'

'Good.'

'I'm not going to pick up a strange man in a bar.'

'Good.'

'And I'm not going to order a male prostitute. Although I still don't see what's so terribly wrong with it.'

'Shall we go over it again?'

'Nah. I'll take your word for it. Anyway, I promised to meet Paula for dinner.'

'She's the depressed friend who complains constantly?'

'Yes. Maybe I should fuck her?'

'But you've always said –'

'That I'm not into women. But I'm thinking if I'm horny enough it won't matter. They say a lot of the guys who give lap dances in gay clubs are straight. Just super-sexed. At a certain point they'll do it with another guy, just to get off. Maybe it'd be like that for me. What do you think?'

'We're all on the spectrum somewhere, with hetero-sexuality at one end and homosexuality at the other.' He shrugged. 'I'm not suggesting it but I'm not vetoing it, either.'

'I don't think I could do Paula.' Nikki shuddered.

'She's too ... lumpy. But there's that new club in town, what's it called? Velvet? Velvet and Iron? Maybe I should check that out?'

'It's Velvet Plus Iron. I believe it's members only. For couples who swing.'

Nikki flashed him a sexy smile. 'In my experience, a super-sexy single woman is always welcome.'

'Tell me about this dinner with Paula. Will it be interminable?'

The rest of the session unfolded smoothly. Nikki compartmentalised her desire for the good doctor by promising herself that, at the conclusion of their final fifty minutes together, which would be soon, she'd kiss his thin, ascetic lips if he didn't kiss her lush, pretty painted lips first. It probably wouldn't happen but it soothed her to think that it might.

'I'll see you next month,' he said as he wrote down their next appointment date and time.

'Great,' she said.

'Keep trying, every day, to spend a wee bit of time in reflection.'

Nikki shivered. She adored his Irish accent, never more so than when he said 'wee'.

'Chilly?'

'No. I just like the way you say "wee".' She batted her lashes. Maybe they'd kiss right now and consider it the end of her therapy?

120

Dr McConnelly blushed again. It gave her a rush even as it silently admonished her. He handed her the appointment card and their fingertips touched. She shivered again. He turned away.

Nikki steered herself out the door and on to the street. God fucking damn, she wanted him. Instead, she faced dinner with Prozac Paula and her lengthy list of woes. Fuck.

For the first half of the meal Nikki practically squirmed in her seat, she was so overdue for a good orgasm. She kept her cell phone on the table, where it passed the evening as it had passed the day – silent. Paula droned on about her mother and her job and her dieting woes. Nikki felt like screaming.

Midway, Nikki abruptly switched gears. It was either that or go mad. Instantly, it was on the tip of her tongue to say, 'Look, Paula, let's just go to your place and make out.' She'd never been with a woman, not even a gorgeous one, so it was a good measure of her desperation that she'd even consider popping her girl/girl cherry with Paula. Nikki easily practised restraint until she could escape.

Good fuck. Good fuck. Good fuck. Nikki's heels tapped out a rhythm to the single phrase that thudded in her head and pulsed in her pussy. She was walking home, too impatient to descend to the subway or try to snag a cab. It was true that she had a rampant libido and that she was disinhibited. But it was also true that she needed a good fuck.

It was easy to understand why she wasn't to fuck any more of her friends' husbands. Harder to understand, really, why she mustn't pick up a stranger. After all, he wouldn't be a stranger for long, would he? Almost impossible to get what was wrong with ordering up a male prostitute. But Dr McConnelly said no. Dr McConnelly said –

The penny dropped. In fact it dropped with such force that, had it been a real penny, it would've been as flat as if it'd been run over by a train. Dr McConnelly said the club was called Velvet Plus Iron. Dr McConnelly said the club was for members only. Now how on earth did her dear old doctor know that?

***

Nikki slid on to a stool at the polished mahogany bar of Velvet Plus Iron. She let her skirt ride up until the tops of her black stay-ups were exposed. She'd undone the top three buttons of her crisp white dress shirt and hung up her jacket. Now she hooked one heel over the foot rail on the bar and smiled at the barkeep. 'A glass of Chardonnay,' she said.

When it arrived she was surprised at the way her hand shook when she picked it up. She was excited, she knew that much. Her pulse was pounding in her ears and her cheeks were hot to the touch. But so excited her hands shook? Perhaps she'd obeyed the dictates of her boundaries for entirely too long. After all, a girl's got to have some fun.

She glanced around from beneath half-closed lids. The club was dark, the tables lit with little lamps and the dance floor illuminated only by spotlights. It was crowded with couples, most of them making out madly. Fuck. It'd been easy to get in but what if she really wasn't welcome here without a mate to swap? What if *he* wasn't here? She'd been so sure he would be she hadn't actually considered –

'Hi.' A tiny, voluptuous redhead leaned on the bar, too close for politeness, which suited Nikki just fine.

'Hi. Um – I don't have a mate so I'm just wondering if it's OK for me to be here.'

'It's certainly OK with me. My name's Amy.' The woman held out her hand.

'I'm, um –' Nikki took her hand. The other woman's palm was small and fleshy in hers.

'You don't have to use your name if you don't want to.' Amy grinned. 'That's my husband over there.' She jerked her head towards a dark corner. The man could be – he leaned into the light to wave. It *was* him.

A wave of relief washed over Nikki, leaving in its wake a desperate desire in her loins, so deep it was almost hard.

Dr McConnelly smiled and mouthed, 'Hi.'

'He's quite a bit older than you,' said Nikki.

'Is that a problem?'

'Not at all.'

'Let's dance.'

Nikki allowed Amy to lead her to the dance floor. The smaller woman took the lead, steering Nikki around with practised ease. Nikki was a bit wooden at first but she relaxed quickly. It was fun.

When Dr McConnelly joined them, he kissed his wife on the mouth, then took over her position, dipped Nikki and kissed her, too.

Nikki was so excited she moaned when their mouths met. Their electricity, connected at last, zapped swiftly through their bodies, leaving her breathless.

'Shall I go up to the room?' Amy asked her husband.

He nodded. 'We'll join you shortly.'

'Yes, sir,' said Amy.

Sir? Doc-tor! Nikki melted into his arms. He pressed her close to his chest and bent his head to nibble her earlobes and neck at his whim, all the while leading her in a series of dances that included the rumba, the cha-cha and a waltz that was a whirl around and around the dance floor that left her panting. Fun!

'Enough foreplay,' he said. 'Come on.'

He led her from the dance floor to an elevator at the far end of the bar.

'What do I call you?' Nikki snagged her jacket from the rack as they rushed past.

'Jack.' He pressed the button and the elevator doors opened. 'Or sir. Depends.'

'Has my therapy officially ended?' Nikki followed him into the car.

'Oh yes.' As the doors closed, he was already gathering her into his arms for another long, breathtaking kiss.

She'd been walking in high heels ever since she'd hit her teens, but as soon as they were inside the hotel room she kicked hers off.

'It's either that or you stop kissing me,' she said apologetically to Jack. 'I'm weak in the knees.'

In response he picked her up and carried her to the king-sized bed, where Amy already reclined, stripped down to her pink bustier and hose. Nikki squealed in genuine surprise, once when Jack effortlessly swooped her off her feet and again when she tumbled on to the bed beside Amy.

'I've never kissed a woman before,' Nikki managed to blurt out before it was no longer true. Amy's mouth was soft on hers and Nikki willingly parted her lips when a curious little tongue tip invited her to. This kiss was familiar in a way, lips on lips, tongue teases and touches, and yet completely opposite to the kisses she'd just enjoyed with Dr – with Jack. Whereas he had possessed her with his mouth, sending shock waves throughout her body, Amy's kiss was a light, delightful sensation, more sensual than sexy, warming Nikki as a comforter might, rather than scorching her from the inside out.

Masculine hands relieved Nikki of her blouse, skirt, bra and panties while feminine caresses kept her distracted. Amy's lips had travelled down her neck and were following her fingers to Nikki's breasts when she felt a strong, lean, decidedly male body press against her from behind.

'Relax,' whispered Jack. 'Lean into me.' He slid his arm under hers and cupped her breast, presenting it to Amy's eager mouth. He hooked his other hand under one of her knees and gently parted her legs, then slid his fingers up her inner thigh until they were pressed against her mound.

Amy nipped and sucked her nipple until it was as hard and pink as the eraser on a pencil. Nikki arched back against Jack, trapping his erection in the cleft of her bum, the tip bumping wetly against the base of her spine.

Jack tortured her with his fingers by gently stroking her pelt without dipping more than the pad of one finger into the slit, making her labia stay furled when Nikki was desperate for them to be splayed.

'Please ...' she whispered, 'help me.'

Jack crooned in her ear. 'You're doing just fine. Be patient.'

'I can't stand it.'

'You can.' He spoke more firmly, in a stern manner she'd never heard before. 'You will.'

'Yes ... sir,' she whispered. The subservience of it sent a thrill through her, instantly replaced by a fierce desire to find out what disobedience would incite. 'Amy, gorgeous Amy, please suck my clit just exactly as you've sucked my nipple, I need to –'

Amy's surprised look blurred as Nikki was swiftly tilted to expose her ass to the air. Before she could draw a breath, the hand that had caressed her pussy with infinite care came down hard on one cheek and then the other, the sound as surprising and sharp as the pain.

'Wait! I'm not ready!' Nikki struggled against his other arm, now firmly pressed against her chest so that her upper back was pinned to his chest while her bottom was left free to wiggle and blush with each blow.

'You're way past ready, girl,' he muttered. He raised his hand higher, which resulted in a harder, louder smack.

Nikki didn't struggle long; it was pointless and the blows that missed their mark due to her movement hurt more than the ones that landed on the plumpest part of her ass. Besides, she found she couldn't catch her breath and when she finally did she started to moan, because by then her ass was on fire and the heat had somehow ignited a flame in her clit.

'Are you going to behave?' Jack still spanked her, as strong and steady as ever.

'Yes. Yes!'

'Do what you're told?'

'I promise!'

Still the spanking continued. Nikki soared completely past pain to pleasure ... then back to pain. The salty taste of tears wet her lips.

Amy leaned in to lick them from her cheeks. 'Sir,' she whispered.

'I promise to be good, sir!' Nikki shrieked.

'All right then,' he said. The beating stopped as abruptly as it had begun. Jack released Nikki and she collapsed back against him once more.

'Amy, why don't you lick this little slave's pussy?' Once again, Jack parted Nikki's knees with his hand. This time, instead of a maddening little stroke, Nikki felt the tip of Amy's tongue circle the circumference once, twice, three times before it started lapping at her clit.

'Oh, God, oh thank you, sir,' mumbled Nikki. She ground her fiery ass against his rigid length, not caring, in fact enjoying, the pain it caused. She was desperate. Not for cock, but for *his* cock.

Jack hitched up behind her and a moment later the rubbery head nudged her slick pussy lips apart. He jerked up hard, sinking the first few inches of his manhood into her aching hole.

Instantly, she began to moan.

The second thrust introduced another few inches. With

128

each subsequent stroke, Jack's cock travelled further up her tunnel, stretching it to fit. And Amy's tongue still circled her clit, her lips now wrapped around it like a second sheath.

It was good, so good to have her cunt perfectly attended to at last. Of course it would take two people, one sucking her clit and one fucking her hole, to do it right. Of course one should be a girl, same as her, non-threatening, helpful even, and the other should be a man, a stern, hard man with a firm hand to make a girl behave. Of course.

Nikki's pussy was as hot, now, as her punished bum. Her need for release reached the boiling point. The orgasm rushed like steam through her body, scorching her nerves and making her shriek. It would kill her before it made good its escape!

'Stop!' She didn't mean it as an order; it was a plea. But it was ignored by her two new lovers. The woman in front kept lapping at her clit while the man behind thrust faster and deeper, fucking her through the scary, scalding part of the orgasm and into the part where it gentled to a rolling boil.

Finally, when Nikki was little more than a limp, occasionally shuddering shape on the bed, they relented and withdrew.

She watched as Jack's cock disappeared between the cheeks of his curvy wife's undulating ass. It didn't shock her that he smacked Amy's bum a dozen times, plundering it all the while, before he reached around to make her climax. She was a little surprised at how loud he was when he came, not at all surprised at the extent of Amy's ecstasy.

'Now for a wee nap,' Jack said. 'When we wake up, you'll return Amy's gift of oral sex and give me one of your infamous blow jobs.'

'Yes, sir,' said Nikki.

'If everything works out,' he said, 'Amy and I just might keep you.'

'Oh?' Now this was a big surprise.

'Uh-huh,' said Amy. 'We're done with swapping, Nikki. We'd like a third to share with each other and some of our good friends.' She gave Nikki a big wet kiss and cuddled up against her. Jack spooned her from behind.

It should have felt strange, but, as Nikki drifted into a dreamless sleep, she felt right at home.

A Trip to the Woodshed
A Lucy Salisbury Story
by Penny Birch

Every girl knows what happens down at the woodshed. Every girl who likes to be spanked, that is. When the time is right your husband takes you by the hand and leads you down the garden. Into the woodshed you go and the door is locked behind you. Over you go, maybe across a trestle, maybe over his knee, but always with your bottom lifted so that it becomes the most prominent part of your body. Up comes your skirt and down come your panties, or maybe you're obliged to wriggle a pair of tight blue jeans down your thighs before you get your knickers pulled down, or maybe you have to strip stark, baby naked. One way or another you end up with a bare bottom, which is then spanked, because that's what happens to girls down at the woodshed. They get their bottoms spanked.

It's one of those perennial fantasies, like having to do a striptease in some sleazy pub, or sucking a lorry driver off in return for a lift, one of those fantasies that proper, sensible girls find utterly horrifying, but which girls like me adore. Just to hear the word 'woodshed' is enough to get me going, triggering daydreams of stern, uncompromising men, the smell of resin and varnish in the hot air, the feel of rough boards under my bare feet and cool air on my bare bottom, the agonising shame of submission to a spanking and the stinging pain of his hand across my naked, bouncing rear cheeks. I love it all, and the man hadn't merely used the word woodshed in some irrelevant context, he'd said, 'what she needs is a trip down to the woodshed'.

He hadn't been referring to me, fortunately, or my pink-cheeked embarrassment would probably have been so strong I'd have risked giving the game away on the instant. I'd merely overheard him use the phrase to a colleague in reference to Gemma Cranes, one of our juniors. She was fresh out of Oxford, smart, sharp and completely self-confident, also beautiful in a rather reserved fashion, with her petite figure, pert little nose and glasses, while she wore her long dark hair piled into a coquettishly loose bun on the back of her head. I could well see that any dominant man would feel that she'd benefit from a swift trip across his knee, in the woodshed or elsewhere, with or without a reason.

In this case there was ample reason. He was head of the company doing the catering at the course on international management techniques Gemma and I were attending. Her comments on the quality of the lunch he'd provided had been biting, loud and delivered in front of several members of his own staff. No wonder he'd thought of punishing her, and, if there was no woodshed to hand, it would have been fine to see her upended in the middle of the cafeteria, her bottom exposed in front of the rest of us, then well spanked as she was given a lecture on manners.

It wasn't going to happen. You can't go around spanking naughty girls at random just because they happen to deserve it, unfortunately, because I would have loved to have watched almost as much as I'd have loved to get the same humiliating treatment for myself. Not that I wanted her hurt, but I wasn't immune to the way her round little bottom moved under her skirt. In fact, I'd have loved to be done side by side with her, cuddled up together in a vain attempt to reduce each other's pain and humiliation as our bottoms were stripped and spanked and maybe even fucked, both of us secretly enjoying every awful moment of our ordeal, but it was never going to happen.

You just can't get away with that sort of thing in an

office environment. People talk, and besides, although Gemma was always friendly, and even seemed to look up to me, she'd done nothing to suggest any lesbian tendencies, let alone masochistic ones. As for the man, I didn't know him at all, and until that moment he'd been just another anonymous face among the dozens I meet every day in my job.

What he'd said changed everything. He was a spanker, or at least he liked the idea of giving Gemma a spanking, and if Gemma, then why not me? When it comes to ordinary sex I can take it or leave it, and when it's office sex I always leave it, but spanking is another matter. I love to be spanked, and I love to be spanked properly, in the classic style, bare bottom over the knee of a man who's fully in charge. I'd never been taken down to a woodshed for punishment either, but I'd always wanted to be, and from the moment I heard him use those words my need for the treatment had grown a hundred times stronger.

I tried to put the idea out of my head, by masturbating myself silly over a dozen variations of the fantasy, but that only made it worse, to the point at which I was wondering if I dared break my rule of keeping business and pleasure separate by finding out who he was and propositioning him. After all, he didn't know who I was, and wouldn't even need to know which company I was with, or that I was with any company at all for that matter. I'd simply be a girl he'd met, supposedly by accident, a girl who appreciated his dark, mature good looks, a girl who liked to be spanked.

Yet there was obviously a chance of another meeting at work, so the project wasn't entirely without risk. In my company, reputation is everything, and if the facts got out I would lose mine. Casual encounters were all very well, but there's a world of difference between sharing a night of passion and asking a man for a bare-bottom spanking. Then there was the issue of my being PA to the big boss, and the terms of my contract, which included not doing anything likely to bring the company into disrepute, a clause that no doubt covered begging for spankings, but I did need my trip down to the woodshed.

I'd quickly decided it wouldn't do any harm to find out who he was, which was a simple matter of making a few innocent enquiries. One phone call and a few minutes on the internet, all entirely above board, and I'd discovered that the centre at which the course had been held had a contract with Redman Catering, and that my man was Mr Redman himself. Even the name was intriguing, making me think of the red flush of a spanked girl's cheeks, both those on her face and on her bottom.

Having found out who he was, it was more than I could resist to discover where he lived and, having done that, to take a look at his house on my computer. The street-level view showed a modest suburban villa, one of hundreds like it in Whitton, which I'd never heard of at all. There was a middling-sized saloon car parked outside and he grew roses, which he kept neatly pruned, all very ordinary. The view from above showed a red tiled roof and an equally neat back garden, all completely mundane, save for one crucial detail, a detail that set my heart racing. At the bottom of the garden was a large square shed.

I knew I was being silly, but I've always had an over-active imagination and the revelation that Mr Redman owned what was effectively a woodshed turned what had already been a strong need into a desperate yearning. It had been far too long since I'd been spanked, or had any of that sort of fun at all, and I needed it badly. Even then I probably wouldn't have had the courage to go through with it, but for a chance discovery.

The internet at work was monitored and strictly controlled, but my phone allowed me to make occasional guilty forays into the world of naughty websites. Mr Redman had brought my need for a spanking to an almost painful peak, and it was more than I could resist not to watch other girls getting it, for all that the experience was as frustrating as it was exciting. One clip showed a petite, red-haired girl jogger being spanked over the bonnet of a car by an irate motorist, but it wasn't the sight of her shorts being pulled down to bare her bottom that fascinated me, or even the thought of her humiliation at the way the lips of her cunt bulged out between her thighs as she was punished, but the car. It was Mr Redman's car.

I had to check very carefully before I could be sure I was right, but it was exactly the same model, in the same colour, and more importantly there was an identical scrape of white paint on one bumper. The number plate was fuzzed out, but it had to be his car, and, while the motorist doing the spanking was another woman, if they were using his car he had to be involved, and was presumably the cameraman. Mr Redman not only enjoyed spanking girls, he was also actively involved in the world of spanking, which not only meant that if I went to him I'd get what I wanted, but also that he'd almost certainly be very discreet.

It still took an awful lot of courage to make the trip to Whitton, but I did it, the following Sunday, in skin-tight jeans that made the best of my bottom and a pair of full white panties beneath, an outfit designed to appeal to my prospective spanker. I nearly turned back several times on the way, and as I approached the house I was telling myself I'd just walk past, that he wasn't likely to be in, that he probably had a wife and children, anything to excuse myself. Only he was in the front garden, admiring his roses, and as he looked up I found the line I'd been rehearsing all the way from the city spilling from my lips.

'Mr Redman? I've been sent for a trip to the woodshed.'

He stood up, surprised but not astonished, his naturally stern gaze flicking from my face to my hips. I knew what he wanted to see and quickly turned around, briefly presenting him with my bottom.

He threw a cautious glance to either side, then nodded. 'You'd better come indoors then, young lady. What's your name?'

I had that ready. 'Emily.'

'Well then, Emily, is this your first time?'

'No.'

I was red-faced as I made my admission, but he took it in his stride, holding the door for me. The inside of his house was as normal as the exterior, but that made my impending spanking all the more exciting. Dungeons and elaborate equipment are all very well, but this was going to be domestic, a naughty girl spanked because she needed it, because it was necessary. He glanced at his watch as he led me through the house, to where a pair of patio doors stood open to the trim little garden at the back, with the square brown shape of the woodshed beyond. I was shaking badly as I followed him across the lawn, but he seemed completely relaxed, as if spanking strange girls half his age was an everyday occurrence.

Even at the door of the shed he showed no great emotion, but unlocked it and ushered me inside. It wasn't as I'd expected, with no piles of chopped logs, heaps of cobwebbed flowerpots or rusting garden implements, just the four plain walls and a number of chairs, set out to the sides, save for one, which stood at the exact centre. That I understood. It was the chair he sat on to dish out his spankings, and, if the presence of the others implied that those spankings were sometimes given in front of an audience, that didn't concern me, for all that it was an exciting thought.

He spoke up once more. 'Right, young lady, let's give you a little time to think about what's going to happen to you. Stand here, that's right, with your bottom towards the end wall. Put your hands on your head. Right, I'll be back in five minutes.'

It was more like fifteen, but I stayed as I was, allowing the apprehension to build in my head, exactly as he intended. I was about to be spanked, almost certainly bare bottom, and by a complete stranger, an unbearably shameful, hideously undignified fate, and one I needed so badly it was making me feel weak. Despite that, I found myself wondering if he had really left me purely in order to ensure that I was feeling thoroughly sorry for myself before my spanking began, or if he had some more sinister purpose. Yet I knew who he was, and my researches had revealed nothing unusual about his character, save that he loved to spank girls on their bare bottoms.

139

I put the thought from my mind, and when he eventually came back he had put a jacket and tie on, making him seem sterner still, the ideal spanker for me. There was no further waiting, no small talk. He knew what to do with me and that was that, sitting down on the central chair with his knees stuck out and speaking as he patted his lap. 'Over you go then, Emily. I'll give you a warm-up, then we'll get down to business.'

I went, lost to the fantasy I'd been building up for so long as I laid myself down across his lap. He did it perfectly, utterly matter of fact as he reached under my belly to unfasten my jeans and tugged down my zip, as if stripping girls for punishment were the most natural thing in the world. I lifted my bottom to make it easier for him, finding it far easier to give in than I'd expected, simply because he took it all so casually. Down came my jeans, tugged over my hips, and I was showing him my knickers in spanking position, a shameful experience by any standards, but one that now seemed completely appropriate.

He gave me a single playful slap, then began to stroke my bottom through my panties, and to talk to me. 'You'll do nicely, very nicely indeed, and I'm glad you had the sense to wear some spanking panties. Not that they're going to be staying up very long, but I do like to see a well-presented bottom before it's stripped. How old are you?'

'Twenty-two.'

'I'd have guessed younger, but never mind, let's start with a belated birthday spanking on your panties before they come down, shall we?'

He began to spank me and I closed my eyes in bliss. I'd expected it to be rougher, more of a punishment, with my knickers whipped straight down along with my jeans and my bottom smacked hard, but there was no denying that the casual dirty way he was handling me was working. I'd known from the start that I was likely to end up on my knees with a cock in my mouth, and I'd been willing to do it for the sake of my spanking, but as he applied the twenty-two firm, well-spaced smacks to the seat of my panties that willingness was turning to an active need.

After the twenty-second smack, he began to rub my bottom again, his fingers lingering on my cheeks and pushing down to press my panties into my slit as he spoke up. 'So pretty, so pretty, in fact, that it's almost a shame to pull them down, almost.'

As he finished, he'd taken hold of the waistband of my panties, to ease them slowly down over my bottom. My head was already full of delicious, dirty shame, but it grew stronger by far as my rear view was exposed, and not only my bare cheeks, but also the tightly knotted little hole between and the pouted lips of my distinctly wet cunt. He realised, even as the sticky panty material

141

was peeled off my sex lips, and gave an amused chuckle for his discovery. 'Well now, I can see you're not just in it for the money!'

I wasn't sure what he meant, but could only guess he assumed I got paid for appearing in spanking porn online. That was a natural enough assumption in the circumstances, but deeply humiliating. With that I wondered if he was expecting to pay me once he'd finished with me and my feelings of shame grew stronger still. To be taken down to the woodshed and spanked was bad enough, a favourite fantasy I'd now realised, but to discover that I'd prostituted myself would make the experience stronger by far and realise a second fantasy.

One thing was for sure. He had no doubt whatsoever about his right to touch me up, his fingers loitering between my open bottom cheeks to explore my anus and the lips of my cunt as he went on. 'Yes, very wet, and very pretty. I do love a neatly turned little cunt, and I don't think I've ever seen such a kissable bumhole.'

I gasped as he suited action to words, spreading my cheeks with his thumbs as he bent down to plant a single firm kiss on my anus. He merely laughed, adjusted my body over his lap as he sat upright once more, and my spanking had begun. Before, he'd been gentle, but this was the real thing, a proper punishment delivered to my bare bottom, the way a naughty girl ought to be spanked. It hurt like anything, making me kick my legs and shake my hair, hating every moment of it even as my excitement rose higher and higher still.

He was a real bastard about it, smacking the back of my thighs and my hips, pausing occasionally to spread my cheeks for a peep at my bumhole or to cup my cunt in his hand and give me a rub. When he stuck a thumb up my hole, I burst into tears of raw shame, at which he asked if I was all right, but I was quickly assuring him I was fine and sticking my bottom up for more. I got it, a long hard spanking, until my whole bottom seemed to be on fire and I'd lost all track of how many smacks had been delivered to my bouncing rear cheeks, while he'd reduced me to a state of wretched, tear-streaked arousal, pathetically grateful for what had been done to me and willing to pleasure him any way he wanted in return.

What I got was a mouthful of cock. Long before the spanking was over I'd been able to feel his erection pressing to my flesh and I had no doubt whatsoever he'd want it attended to. The moment he let go of me I was on my knees, my trousers and panties still in a tangle around my legs as I jerked my top and bra up to show off my tits. He seemed a little surprised, but made no effort to stop me as I unzipped him and pulled out his cock and balls, first to tug at his lovely thick shaft, then to pop as much of it into my mouth as I could get and set to work at sucking him off.

It wasn't the first time I'd given a man a blow job to say thank you for a spanking, and I made a point of keeping my red-hot bottom well thrust out so that he could admire the view as I worked on his erection. I also wanted to come, and my fingers were soon between my legs, fiddling with my cunt as I played over what he'd done to me in my head. My woodshed fantasy was always a punishment, and he'd spanked me purely for our mutual pleasure, but aside from that it was perfect. I'd been taken down the garden, knowing what I was going to get in advance. I'd been turned over a man's knee and had my jeans and panties pulled down, gradually, so that I was forced to savour every humiliating moment of my exposure. I'd been spanked, bare bottom, until I'd begun to cry, and to add one final, awful detail, he'd touched me up while he spanked me.

I came, gulping on his cock as my orgasm ran through me, hard and long, with my fingers slapping on my soaking cunt as I masturbated him into my mouth. No man takes that for long, and I was still coming as his cock erupted down my throat, making me gag and filling my mouth with hot salty spunk before I could pull away, only to get the second spurt full in my face and the third all over my top and tits.

That was it, done, and I'd hung my head in shame and exhaustion even before he spoke up, as casual as ever. 'Hang on, I've got a handkerchief.'

He pulled it from his pocket and I began to mop up, blushing and grinning sheepishly as I wiped the spunk from my face and breasts. I felt deeply ashamed of myself, but also happy, and I knew full well that as soon as my need had grown strong again I'd be back, if he wanted me, and that seemed highly likely.

He asked first. 'Was that good?'

'Lovely, thank you. You really know how to spank a girl.'

'So I should, and you're a delight to spank. Come on then, I expect you'd like a glass of wine or something while you watch Jane get hers.'

I was in the act of pulling up my panties and jeans, and quickly finished adjusting myself before I replied, puzzled. 'Jane?'

'You must know Jane. Tiny, copper-coloured hair, bottom like a ripe apricot.'

'Oh, the girl in your video, but what's she doing here?'

Now it was his turn to look puzzled. 'She's next up for the woodshed, of course. Irene's going to spank her, then give her the cane.'

'Irene?'

'My wife.'

We'd been walking up the garden as we spoke, and had now come to the patio. The doors were wide open as before, but the living room was no longer empty. In fact, it was crowded with people, mostly men and of all

145

shapes and sizes; fat ones and thin ones, short ones and tall ones, the young and the old, but every single one of them watching a huge television screen that showed an image of Mr Redman seated on the chair in the woodshed with a girl over his knee, a girl with a bare, well-smacked bottom, her long legs kicking wildly in the air, her blonde hair tossing in her pain, her rounded little bottom cheeks spread to show off her anus and her soaking wet cunt. It was me.

Careful What You Wish For
Willow Sears

'Christ, Willow!' gasped my cousin's husband, trying to look back at me over his shoulder. 'You really *are* a dirty bitch, aren't you?'

Yes, actually, I really *am*.

I was wearing a pair of my black latex gloves, so there was no reason not to get properly intimate. I ran my fingertip along that sure-fire pleasure spot sited at the perineum, the little ridge of skin that ran from his anus to his balls. It never failed. He rather inappropriately grunted the Son of God's name again and I felt his cock swell further in the tight grip of my other hand. His face had lost some of its natural arrogance. The cheeks were flushed and the nose scrunched. He was flustered and on heat, unsettled by my explorations around his most private place, but too macho and too turned on to try to stop me. Some men feel emasculated by any attentions towards their arsehole. They probably think liking it makes them gay. He was clearly nervous of it, but wanted to play the Big Man, the Supreme Fucker of Sexy Girls. I was the sexiest he had ever been with for sure. He didn't want to appear amateur or prudish in my eyes, especially as he thought he had been the one to instigate all this. He wanted to show that he was up for anything. He wanted to prove that he was in my league. Never had he been so wide of the mark.

His original seduction technique had been strangely effective. His wife was chatting intimately to Celeste on the other sofa. I had gone to the kitchen on a mission to down more champagne, and he had followed. He had smilingly cut off my return, placing a hand lightly on my arm to keep me there, with my back to the worktop. He was half-pissed and half-grinning, his mouth slowly opening and closing as if chewing on imaginary gum. I have no idea why he thought this was attractive. Maybe it was a display of cool nonchalance. Like a true connoisseur he swirled his huge brandy around the glass, between little flicks of his head designed to move the dark locks from his steely eyes. Yes, he was forty years old and *still* had a full flowing mane to boast of. My, how manly and suave!

He leaned in towards me and his voice was low and secretive. He gave me some of the usual crap to imply how important and successful he was, then after some general blah-di-blahing he eventually cut to the chase. The talk throughout the evening had been mostly suggestive, so he thought it appropriate to share a few deeper intimacies.

'You're a cock-stiffening little minx,' he said, and I had to admire his faultless character analysis. 'I bet there's not much you don't do between the sheets!'

There was little to say to this so I shrugged and turned back to the counter, ready for more bubbly. He took it upon himself to reach out and give my bum a brief squeeze. I should have punched him square in his smug grinning face, but I didn't. I bit my lip and curbed the instinct to take instant revenge. The shrewdest part of my brain realised that there was potential to be explored here. There was *something* in his self-assured boldness that set the thoughts of sexy possibilities racing. And who am I to deprive myself of such pleasures? So I reached out and gave his crotch a squeeze in return, feeling the almost instant swell beneath my palm. He breathed hard with the welcome shock of it. The grin melted as the fuck-longing spilled through him, replaced by a half-snarl of surging desire. I let him expand uncomfortably until he was squirming beneath my grasp, and then I let him free. He was closer now, his large frame in my personal space and looming over me as he readied to pounce. His face was flushed red and he was almost panting with lust. As always I remained cucumber cool.

149

'Well, you *are* a big boy, aren't you?' I smiled.

'Your arse is fucking gorgeous. I want it. It's driving me up the wall.'

An arse that drives you up walls? Now *there's* an invention crying out for a patent.

'And what do you think your wife would say if she heard you saying such a thing?' I said.

'She needn't know. You know I love her but she's way too frigid to give her arse to me. Don't think I haven't tried. I love sexy backsides and I love fucking them, but it's been so long now I can hardly remember. That's just not on. It's completely unfair. Anyway, I don't want to fuck a flat skinny arse like hers, I want a nice one with a bit of meat on, like yours, one I could really slap against – not fat, just *perfect*.'

I love the way men get so het up when they are feeling horny. It would be fun one day to watch one get so frustrated that he literally exploded in a huge spattering spunky shower – presuming, of course, that I was safely behind some kind of blast-resistant transparent screen.

'And what would you do with my bum if I gave it to you?' I enquired, remaining unperturbed.

'Fill it,' he gabbled. 'Fill it and fuck it until you screamed. I know a filthy whore like you would just love to have her shit-hole stretched open and stuffed, so don't pretend otherwise.'

Well, he sure knew how to charm a lady. He was

saying all the right things – other than the bit about cheating on my cousin, obviously.

'Well, I can see what you and I would get out of this, but what about your wife? I couldn't possibly betray her even if you could. She would have to know, so you would have to make sure she got something equally wonderful in return.'

That's when the idea properly started to form. It had just been jumbled thoughts before, but these suddenly crystallised. He shook his head blankly, trying to imagine what the *something wonderful* could be. So I told him. Celeste. His eyes sprang saucer-wide and he all but dribbled down his shirtfront. The implications were mind-bogglingly exciting, judging by his expression of awe. He instinctively grabbed his own crotch, as if it might leap from his trousers if not held back.

'I want you right now, you sexy-arsed, prick-teasing bitch.'

'And what do you want me for?' I taunted.

'A deep, hard arse-fucking that I will never forget,' he sneered.

It was these dirty words that cemented my decision to give him exactly what he asked for.

'Yes,' I whispered close to his ear, 'I can give you that.'

I side-stepped him and made my escape while he was busy trying to think of obscenities to gabble at me, and before he could pull his straining erection free from his trousers in the hope of committing some atrocity upon me. There would be time for his bare cock another day. First I had to convince his wife that there was a bargain to be struck.

It must be said I *do* partly invite such overt sexual outpourings as his, which you would know if you'd ever seen me in action. Scene-setting and character descriptions are so very boring but I had better fill you in so you know what you are dealing with. Firstly, the scene: a Fucking Big House somewhere in the middle of nowhere in deepest rural England, owned by him and his wife, who just happens to be my cousin. Reason for my presence: two blocks of three nights staying as their guest, since it was way too long a journey for flying visits. The stays were spaced a week apart, the first to attend the hen night, the second the wedding itself of my cousin's younger sister, who, by strange coincidence, is also my cousin. I took Celeste along for the ride. I like to be provocative so it's good to have a sexy girl at my side to give the relatives something to natter about. Anyway, I needed someone to fuck and to carry all my stuff. Celeste was certainly more slave or plaything than girl-friend, but I was fond of her. Her father was Kenyan and her mother French, and I thought her rather exotic. I'm not sure why, although the fact that she was an exotic dancer should have given me a clue. I loved her pristine dark-chocolate skin and most of all her narrow-hipped, big jutting bottom. She loved to be spanked and that was good enough for me.

As for the other *dramatis personae* you need to know of, first and most definitely foremost is me: delicious, bold, ravishing, that sort of thing. Bisexual and true exponent of all things kinky. Long raven hair. Smallish perky tits with delightfully tiny pale nipples. Championship-winning bottom that is nicely full considering my frame. Delectable, tight, hairless quim that very, *very* few people have experienced or will ever get to experience. Sadistic Goddess of BDSM by night, designer of mainly rubber fetish clothing by day. Habitual wearer of said skin-tight garments, hence the reason that men I barely know mistakenly believe it's OK to squeeze my arse without formal invitation. Like I said, provocative.

Next is him: blind to all but his own needs. Rich and proud of it. Tasty Merc on the drive and new-ish wife ten years his junior to stand as proof that wealth equals happiness. The hair and eyes you already know about. Well dressed, flash and arrogant. Handsome in a well-dressed, flashy, arrogant kind of way. Reasonably nice-cocked as cocks go, but I've seen nicer. Full of himself and interminably randy, therefore six foot plus of forever bubbling testosterone. Something else too, more difficult to quantify: while he was on the face of it an intelligent, ingratiating, humorous and charming man, he was also, undoubtedly, more than a bit of a cunt.

Finally comes her, my cousin: funny, slightly scatty, pretty in an English Rose kind of way. Somewhat naive and self-conscious, although prone to bouts of seemingly uncharacteristic boldness (for instance she once, out of the blue, instigated a skinny-dipping free-for-all at a drunken end-of-term beach party). We were very close during some of our younger days and formed quite a bond, despite her being a couple of years older. She saw me through many scrapes and never gave up on me. She probably had a crush on me, but then who wouldn't? In recent years she confided that she was jealous of my open sexuality. In her roundabout blushing way she revealed she may have certain, well, you know ... *tendencies* that she had never given in to but now rather wished she had.

'You mean you've never fucked another girl?' I had said to her, feigning amazement. 'Well, you should. You haven't lived until you have. They are sweet and so wonderfully soft. They are fragrant, juicy and incomparably delicious. And you can do way, way dirtier things with them than you can do with most men! I can't believe you've never even kissed a girl. I always had you down as at least sixty per cent lezzer, maybe even seventy-five. Even when you got married I knew you were only doing it because it was "the done thing" and because he had pots of lovely cash!'

I then launched into one of my enthusiastic lectures on the more specific delights of Sapphic love. She got to sit there silently with her cheeks aflame as I described the wonders of tribbing, of that first wet kiss between two hot quims pressing together, of sucking on a hot soft clit. She chewed upon her bottom lip and squirmed in her seat but I am ever the mischievous girl so I pressed on remorselessly. She got to learn about how lovely it was to squeeze a pair of big bare tits and pinch and stretch the swelling nipples. She had a nice bouncy pair of jugs herself so she knew this bit was aimed at her. She also got to hear in great detail how sexy it was to spank a girl, or to bend her over and tug on her long hair while you very slowly slid your middle finger all the way up her bum.

Without even delving too far into my kinkier antics, I did the trick and left her all hot and bothered and praying for action. I knew I could have had her right there and put her out of her misery. She would have been putty in my hands. I remember briefly toying with the idea of making her strip off and masturbate while I watched, but she was one of my closest allies and I owed her too much to be that cruel. What I did do, rather fortuitously as it turned out, was promise her that one day soon I would make sure she did indeed get to fuck a beautiful girl. I then winked and told her with a giggle that I would very happily fuck her myself if not for the whole sordid incesty thing. I think her heart stopped for a second or two. I wasn't being entirely truthful as it happens. I *do* love her to bits but she isn't quite my type looks-wise and she really is lacking in the rump department. Give me a nice chubby arse any day! The incest bit did kind of turn me on though ...

***

The long and short of it was that, having previously had this conversation with her, it made broaching the old partner-swapping subject so much easier. Thus the night after the wedding I found myself in one bedroom with her husband, while she and Celeste were holed up in another. The difficulty with the husband was never going to be in getting him naked, it was going to be in keeping him under control. As soon as we were alone I laid down the only ground rules that would apply. My ones.

'I don't kiss or do any nonsense lovey-dovey stuff, so don't even think about it,' I said. 'You will only touch me when or if I tell you. I know what you want from me and you will get it, but before that you must do exactly as I tell you, without question. Do you understand?'

He looked back at me with a slow nonchalant smile, just to prove he was only playing along to get his part of the bargain. 'What have we here?' he said slyly. 'A kinky bitch who thinks she's in control. Well, just as long as you're prepared for some hard, dirty arse sex, darling, because we both know that's what I'm after.'

I was indeed prepared.

I was in a tight black catsuit with a chunky zip that ran all the way down the front, right under the crotch and up to the top of my bum. It was a gamble because one swift yank could see me opened like a split peach. I therefore had to lay down the law as quickly as possible. I began with a bit of appeasement, to keep him under the thumb. I let the zip down to my belly button to show off my pale skin and more than a hint of cleavage. My nipples were covered in little black heart pasties, so I was happy for my tits to be fully free if necessary. I then slid my hand slowly down into my catsuit, so he could see it outlined beneath the shiny material. I rummaged around for effect and then brought my hand back out and provocatively sucked upon my middle finger. There isn't a straight man alive who wouldn't do exactly as you told him once he had witnessed that.

Once naked, he would be easier to handle. My command was thus for him to take off his clothes and show me his gorgeous big cock. Again, the words *gorgeous* and *big* were carefully chosen and guaranteed to shave seconds off the stripping time. He undressed and reclined proudly, propping his back against the head-board with his legs out straight and his fine prick already standing up to attention. I searched my ever-present little bag of tricks and came out with a small bottle of oil and a pair of black latex gloves. His smile widened further. Strange how the colour black makes anything so sexy and acceptable, even surgical paraphernalia. I straddled his legs to put the gloves on and then took a hold of his pulsing prick. I strung out a glob of spit to ease down and land upon the tip of his cock. It made him shiver and sigh. Gently, since he was still not fully under my control, I ran my fist up his hard length to slide the foreskin over his glans and coat it with my saliva. I could already see the pre-come oozing from his little hole to aid the process. I increased my wanking pace very gradually, adding drops of oil to keep both shaft and glans well lubricated.

'I bet Celeste has her fingers up inside your wife's sopping wet pussy right now,' I cooed. 'She likes to get them in deep and stir them slowly around so they are completely coated in scrumptious pussy cream. Then she will take them out and smear the juice all over your wife's big tits. She will suck them clean one by one, filling her mouth with your wife's fat swollen nipples. While she is still gorging on them, she will stuff two fingers back up your wife's dripping snatch and fuck her faster and more noisily than you could ever believe.'

His eyes were half-closed and his breathing was hard. Half the battle would be in keeping him focused on other things, to mix the exhilaration of being with someone new with the thought of his wife elsewhere having dirty things done to her by a sexy black bitch. No doubt he had already pondered taking his wife from behind later, after she had spilled the beans. More likely he had assumed that Celeste was also up for grabs, that he might get his chance to plunder her too, spurting right into her bowels as he gripped her muscular thighs and slapped hard against her soft jiggling bottom. I kept his interest peaking with my dirty talk. It was easy for me, since my mind was already filled with the images of my girl and my lovely cousin fucking with wet passion. Slowly, slowly I teased the hormones from his balls to disperse around his body so that he would be mine for the taking. Never rush this process. Play your cards right and any man will reach the point when he will do whatever is required just to spray his spunk. I patiently stroked his cock and squeezed his fat ball sack and talked dirty talk until I could see his eyes open and brighten with lust. Then I knew he was ready for the ruder things.

***

I can't say that swinging is my forte, mainly because I don't usually have a partner to swap around. I have never had a boyfriend. The cocks I have dealings with generally belong to wimpy men who worship me and unthinkingly do as I command. Even my girlfriends are desperate to adhere to my every whim. However, this swapping malarkey did seem the ideal solution in this case. He would be up for it at the drop of a hat, but my cousin would need more persuading. The thought of naughtiness is fine and dandy, but actually cheating on one's partner is another matter. I knew at the heart of swinging lay the desire for naughtiness *with consent*, and a lack of jealousy afterwards. I would have to hatch a plan to ensure this.

Before the end of our first stay I was already dropping my cousin hints about how much Celeste fancied her (this wasn't far wrong, as I subsequently found out, having spanked the truth from my slave). I didn't let on about her husband's designs upon my body. Between the stays I had a long phone chat with her. I told her it was time to make good my promise and get her fucked by a beautiful girl. She was giggling and protesting on the end of the line but I told her I was deadly serious and that Celeste couldn't wait. I gave her a little rundown of all the things my slave had supposedly said she wanted to do to her. My cousin pretended to chide me for being so naughty but I knew her fingers were in her pussy. As a last resort she tamely claimed her husband would never allow it. We both knew he would. I told her I would deal with him and make sure he was out of the way. I said I would sort it so there were no repercussions. I requested his mobile number so I could concoct a phoney reason for him to be missing on the night. However, I didn't do so. What I actually did was send him a text saying *be ready for me at the weekend.*

With the whole thing still a secret between them, there was no chance they would discuss it and therefore no chance for cold feet. Celeste and I returned the next weekend and the flirty stuff continued as before. He was practically turning blue with his need to get me alone. She could barely stand with the leg-wobbling anticipation of having a naked Celeste in her bed. It was immense fun!

I made them wait until our last night there. He was under orders to go along with whatever I said. I came down to dinner in my black catsuit. Celeste had nothing but a leopard-skin-print bodystocking to cover her lovely form. The meal was a smutty affair, driven by my constant suggestive remarks. Over much wine I forced my cousin to admit her fantasy of being fucked by another girl. I also forced her husband to admit that allowing it was the least that he could do. I related some true tales of rudeness from the fetish clubs I go to. I made them talk about favourite positions. I even made him tell me about his cock. For one minute I thought he was so pent up he was going to whip it out and try to toss it off all over me from the opposite side of the table. When the clearing up was being done I got my cousin alone and told her it was all arranged. I said I would stay with her husband to give her and Celeste time alone. He had agreed it would be his present to her. I told her I might give him a little thank-you treat, but it would be nothing that would ever cause friction between them, nor anything that would stop him wanting her just as much as before.

'If he allows you this,' I said, 'he will always want something in return. I will make you evens. Don't worry – I have a knack of making a very little seem like an awful lot.'

The subject was thereafter not up for discussion. The girls had champagne, he poured himself a vast brandy and we adjourned to the lounge. Celeste gave an impromptu display of her exotic dancing, firstly for us all, then mainly for my cousin. When Celeste wiggles her barely covered behind at you then slowly pushes it out towards your face, it's a very strong will that manages to turn down a golden chance to fuck with her. I led him away to ensure there was no possibility of this. I guess the sound of the door closing behind us must have been the sweetest my cousin had ever heard. Imagine, the force of all those years of longing and desire, all rushing through you in a single instant. The thought of her joy was almost heart-bursting. You see? I *can* be good. But then straight away I had some more badness to attend to.

* * *

Once I had stroked his cock good and proper I dismounted to select a couple of utter corkers from my toy collection. First was a rather bizarre, almost medieval-looking instrument of sublime torture. It was ostensibly a paddle, having a small tongue in thin plastic protruding from one end, but then it had a long black feather sprouting from the other. The other was the most unprepossessing but ingenious bit of kit I have ever seen. It was totally benign in appearance; little more than a thin white cord with an adjustable loop at its centre and two more at either end. Nowt worrisome about that, you might think. The middle loop I used to carefully place around his ball sack, telling him that I didn't want him going off too early. As I pulled the ends a little the middle loop tightened slightly around his tubes, restricting any outward-bound flow of spunk and pulling the skin tight over his bulging testes to give them a smooth shine. I ran my fingertips over them to show that this restriction had actually made his balls even more sensitive. I then began to lightly spank his balls with the paddle – just tiny taps to take his breath away and to cause his erect prick to strain further. That's how I managed to get him to turn over.

I eased him on to his side, moving his upper leg away from me, so that his bollocks were stuck out behind him between his thighs, like a bulldog's. I gave him a few more little slaps and then brought the feather into action, tickling around his balls and perineum, and very lightly over his anus. His inhibitions were falling away. As I reached around to grasp his prick with my still-lubricated still-gloved hand, he pushed his arse out at me to open himself up to the feather tip. I let him have it, a tiny brush over the centre of his arsehole.

'Christ, Willow!' he gasped. 'You really *are* a dirty bitch, aren't you?'

I put down the feather/paddle and let my fingers do the talking. I was holding his prick tight to feel its pulse, and running the fingertips of my other hand all around his perineum. Then, very slowly, I began to wank him once more. My greased fingers were around his arse but the thumb would be the easiest for insertion. He knew what was going to happen. He might have been dying to say no but he just couldn't make himself. I made to ease him on to his front and he complied. Just one more move to go. I pushed forward with my thumb and gently pushed at his entrance. He closed up tight instinctively. I heard him exhale in a rush, perhaps relieved, perhaps embarrassed that his arse had taken such a stance against me. I told him to raise his hips and he did. Still slowly I pushed and then suddenly he relented, his anus relaxing so my thumb could slide inside. There followed some more gasping, more calling me a dirty bitch and taking God's name in vain. I was nearly there. I reached around for his prick again but couldn't toss him with his hips only slightly off the bed.

'I need you on your knees,' I said quietly.

It must have cost his machismo dearly to comply, but he wordlessly did so. Still with my thumb up inside him he manoeuvred first on to one knee and then the other, pushing his rump out at me so I could wiggle my thumb inside him closer to his sensitive gland. I had him now, for sure. I stopped tossing him and gave his balls more attention. I squeezed them and tugged gently at the strings still restricting his spunk. I could pull them outwards between his legs and spit on them. I could slap them from side to side between his thighs while I wiggled my thumb up his arse. All this he seemed to love, although he was still stupidly insisting on calling me a kinky bitch and a whore, which, let's face it, was at least partially the reason he was in so much trouble in the first place. While he was preoccupied with my wiggling thumb, I slipped the looped ends of the strings around each foot in turn, and pulled them to tighten at his ankles. Now he was definitely mine.

The genius of this little piece of string apparatus could now be fully appreciated. The middle loop pulled tight around his bollocks and the ends were tight around his ankles. He couldn't move. Raise his hips higher and it would mean castration. Move a leg and the same fate awaited him. Even reaching back was no good. The ties could not now be eased back over his feet without pulling his sack clean off. He couldn't loosen the loop around his balls as that was dependent on first freeing the ones at his feet, and we know what trying to do that resulted in. All this I carefully related to him as he stared incredulously at my smirking face. Move a muscle, I told him, and be prepared to sing soprano.

'Don't worry,' I said, 'you will still get what you asked for. You just have to be a good boy and stay patient.'

He didn't seem convinced but I'm not one to break my word. However, firstly I had to explain that no one called me a bitch or a whore and got away with it, and no one but no one squeezed my arse without my say-so. He still wasn't learning. In fact, *bitch* seemed to be his current favourite word, especially after a little jerk of his ankle demonstrated my recent point about castration perfectly. I thought the best thing all round was to place a bulldog clip on his tongue. He could try to speak and call me names but it would only hurt him.

'Don't touch it, darling,' I told him cheerfully, 'or I might have to pull your bollocks off.'

I brought my bag of tricks over and let him see me take out the carefully chosen dildo. It was thin and smooth but very long. It was made out of hard plastic but it carried a tube through its centre so that an oozy spunk-like goo could be sent through it to squirt from the end. His arse was already well lubed from my thumb's insertion, so he was good to go, although from his panicky, bulldog-clip-restricted sounds of objection you'd think he wasn't as up for it as he had previously claimed.

'You said you wanted me,' I reminded him, careful to use his exact words, 'for a deep, hard arse-fucking that you wouldn't forget. Well, here it comes!'

He did wriggle a bit but the pull on his ball sack soon taught him the wisdom of remaining still. I placed the tip of the dildo against his hole and eased forward to spread him. My thumb had loosened him amply. There was no resistance this time. I maintained a slow forward slide as I relentlessly buried the thin shaft inside him. His head dropped and he gave out a low moan, but having reached round to clasp his cock I found it hard as iron. I pressed patiently on until all eight or nine inches had been taken in by his greedy arse. He didn't need much more preparation. I gripped his cock and used it as a handle to gain purchase as I thrust in and out. He had specified a deep fucking, so I made sure to stick my bottom right out to withdraw as fully as possible before driving home again. I gave a squeeze on the rubber bulb to send a first spray of cool ooze through the centre of the toy and out inside him. It would keep him nice and slippery as I increased my pace and power. I gripped the base of his rigid prick and wanked swiftly at it, my fingers bashing at his tied-off balls. Slowly I wrenched the pent-up spunk through his restricted tubes to amass at the base of his shaft in readiness for its final journey. I was careful to keep my furious wanking as close to his balls as I could. I didn't want to send his spunk careering off down his ready cock too soon.

His arse was fully relaxed so I soon got a lovely fast rhythm going. I didn't even have to wank him, as each thrust now jarred his prick through my tightly encircling, greased fingers. It meant that I could concentrate on using my free hand to pull his hair, to slap his back and outer thighs, to pinch and punch his buttocks. I chucked in a few insults for good measure, calling him a *bitch* and a *whore* just to see how he liked it. I am proud of my stamina and gave him a real good, long shagging – not like those girls you see in films who give up or lose the rhythm after mere minutes. I slowed only to free his ankles and bollocks from the constraining cord. When he came I wanted a huge onrush that ripped along his prick, burning his tubes and erupting with scalding force. His prick would need very little encouragement. I slid forward one last time until my thighs were squashing his arse flat. I gave a few quick hard squeezes on the rubber bulb and the remainder of the spunk goo was sent shooting out to fill and sluice his bowels. Then I moved my grip from the base of his cock to the middle. Ensuring that the dildo was as deep inside him as possible, I then gave him the fastest, slickest wank of his life. The previously inert semen was drawn into a sudden stampede down his shaft. He squealed a little bit like a girl when the first spurt shot messily from his twitching prick-head, but I kept tossing him as fast as before despite my mirth. Each forward jerk of my fist brought another gooey wad and each emission sounded like it cost him more dearly. He must have sprayed eleven or twelve separate blasts from his jerking shaft and it was as much mess as I've ever seen from a single prick.

When I slipped out of him he stayed on his knees with his face buried in the bed sheets. I told him for a final treat I would leave him to privately expel, with a shiver-inducing purge, the mass of goo from inside him. I freed him from the bulldog clip but he had no words for me. I told him I was going. I told him I would not tell his wife about what I had done to him. It would be our little secret forever, his reward for letting my cousin have such a sexy black-arsed Celestial treat. I promised not to reveal a word, unless he embellished at all about our coupling. He was to tell her that I hadn't removed a single item of clothing, nor had he touched me at all. I suggested he be content to tell her that I simply gave him the most incredible, most bollock-wrenching hand-job of his life, which was of course completely true.

I entered the girls' room as quietly as possible so as not to distract them. My cousin had Celeste's fat bum squashed down on her face, so she was never going to notice my arrival. My girlfriend's chocolate rump shone with spit and pussy juice. Her quim, when it lifted from my cousin's stuck-out tongue, was dripping its lovely cream. I unstrapped the dildo at my crotch and unzipped my catsuit fully so I could get my hand inside to clutch my bare quim. I watched for a while as they took turns to lick, suck and finger each other's holes. Celeste was a good girl and gave my cousin good encouragement to be as dirty as she liked. They had obviously made each other come a good few times and both sported fuck-happy smiles. My cousin only spotted me after she let her head droop backwards following another hard clit-sucking and a sharp climax. She gave me a big smile of gratitude and held out her hand, wanting me to join the fun. Perhaps I should have but I resisted. Instead, I handed Celeste the dildo in its harness. I gave instructions and my cousin was readied with spit and lube and then pierced by the long plastic toy. Very slowly and gently my cousin had her little virgin arse beautifully fucked. It was clearly the highlight of her evening, maybe even of her life. Afterwards I sent her dazed but euphoric back to her husband, so that I could at last enjoy a few bitch-induced climaxes of my own.

* * *

I tried to slip out early and unnoticed in the morning but he caught me as Celeste was loading my car. He was already on heat, all jittery and drooling like he could barely contain himself. Unbelievably, he was *still* sneering and calling me a kinky whore! Would he *never* learn his lesson? I just shrugged and waved away his gibbering nonsense, so he put his hand into the opening of his pyjamas and hauled out his cock. It was already hard and he was thrusting his hips out and pointing it at me as if it was a gun and I was supposed to freeze and put my hands up. Then he was frenziedly tugging away at it, like he wanted to tear it off and throw it at my head. If it wasn't for the strange leering grin plastered across his face, I might have been genuinely worried for his sanity.

'This isn't over, you prick-teasing little bitch!' he said, still tossing himself. 'One day I *will* have your sexy bitch arse, just you wait and see!'

Just the talk and the thought of it was enough and his prick was suddenly jerking and sending spunk-bombs shooting across the kitchen in my direction. I had seen enough. I stuck my bottom out at him, blew him a taunting kiss over my shoulder and left him with the words, 'Be careful what you wish for!'

I already knew what I would do to him in the unlikely event I agreed on another swapping session, and boy was he in for a surprise!

Loser Takes All
Amber Leigh

'Strip poker,' cried Cassidy. 'I want us all to play strip poker.'

They were the words that changed everything.

She made the exclamation just as Nickelback's 'Rockstar' had finished playing. In the silence following the final strains of the track – a rock concert audience chanting the refrain of the song – Cassidy's cry hung in the air like the raunchiest challenge imaginable.

Strip poker.

Beth shivered and couldn't decide whether she was excited by the idea or simply horrified. John stiffened. Ray glanced quizzically in Cassidy's direction.

Beth held her breath.

The air had already turned thick with electricity. The

moment was so quiet she could hear fingertips of rain caressing the cottage's windows. Now, Beth knew, it was a matter of seeing who responded first to Cassidy's suggestion. And then, of course, it would be a matter of seeing how that person responded.

She had thought the holiday was turning out to be a huge disappointment. Admittedly, the cottage she and Ray had rented with their best friends was clean, cosy and comfortable. But they'd expected summer sunshine and enough warm weather to enjoy the occasional moonlight swim in the nearby lake. Because of the constant rain, the four of them had spent their days stuck inside the cottage playing card games, drinking lager and listening to John's extensive collection of illegally downloaded rock albums. The only times they seemed to have left the cottage had been when they were making a rushed journey to the nearby supermarket to top up on essential supplies.

'Come on,' Cassidy pressed. She held up the battered deck of cards they had been using over the past two days. It was a deck they had found in one of the cottage's many cupboards and drawers. 'Who's up for a game of strip poker?'

'I'm in,' Ray said, shrugging.

Beth stared at him with undisguised surprise. Since when had her husband shown any interest in poker? Let alone strip poker?

John grunted and tossed down the book he'd been reading. He made a laboured show of appearing relaxed about the invitation, as though he played strip poker most nights of the week and it was somewhere between a bothersome hobby and a nuisance chore. But Beth noticed the sly glance he stole in her direction. She could sense he was concealing a desperate urge to play the game.

'Go on then,' John said with forced ease. 'I'll play a couple of hands.'

Cassidy clapped her hands. 'That's three of us playing,' she chirped. 'What about you, Beth? Are you in?'

The question sent a spasm of liquid excitement rippling through the muscles of Beth's sex. She glanced up at her best friend and saw the shine of something sly and sexual in Cassidy's eyes. John and Ray were studying her with cool and curious calm. It seemed as though the future of their communal happiness in the holiday cottage depended on her response.

'Strip poker?' Beth asked carefully. 'Are you three serious? Do you really want to play that?'

'I'll deal you a place,' said Cassidy.

And that was all it took.

John sorted fresh drinks for everyone – beer for the boys and alcopops for the girls – while Ray retrieved a tray of nibbles he had prepared earlier. If Beth hadn't known better, she would have thought the three of them had planned for this moment. She dismissed the paranoid thought and selected another rock album on John's iPod while the others took their places, sitting cross-legged on the floor around the cottage's square coffee table.

Trying to make the gesture appear innocent, Beth shrugged her arms into a convenient fleece before joining the other three. It wasn't cheating, she assured herself. It was merely an insurance policy against her own lack of familiarity with the rules of poker.

Cassidy dealt and snapped instructions as though she was a croupier from a Vegas casino. Beth suspected a lot of Cassidy's knowledge came from the Texas Hold 'Em game on her BlackBerry, but it would have been churlish to point that out.

'The winner of each hand gets to name the loser,' Cassidy explained. 'And the winner gets to tell the loser which item of clothing to remove.'

John and Ray nodded.

Beth said nothing, sure the mounting excitement was going to make her faint. They were sitting boy-girl-boy-girl around the table. She reached slyly to her right and found Ray's hand. His fingers slid between hers and gave a reassuring squeeze. It was the pressure of those fingers against hers that made her realise, whatever happened this evening, it would all be all right. Ray was there for her and she was there for him.

Beth snatched her hand away once Cassidy had dealt

the cards. She stared in dismay at a seven and a three. Bids, bets, raises, checks and calls were made quickly. Community cards were flopped on to the table. And, because no one had anything worth gambling on, John won the hand by default.

'Pick someone,' Cassidy urged. 'Pick a loser. Tell them what clothes to remove.'

His smile was tight. He glanced at Beth and she could see an appraising shine in his eyes that had never been there before.

Her heart skipped a beat when she realised Cassidy's attractive husband was giving her a bold admiring glance. He was contemplating asking her to remove an item of clothing. The idea was so exciting it made her chest tighten. Involuntarily, the muscles in her thighs stiffened.

John's gaze never left Beth.

Her pulse quickened. She was making seductive eye contact with her best friend's husband. And she was doing that while her own husband sat immediately by her side. The heat in her loins was molten.

She watched John's lips part as he said, 'Take off your top, Cassidy.'

Beth released a heavy sigh. She couldn't decide whether she was overwhelmed by relief or disappointment.

Cassidy rapped her knuckles lightly against John's bicep. 'You bastard. Why me?'

He snatched his gaze away from Beth. His grin never faltered. 'You were the one who suggested this game. I figured you should make the first forfeit.'

She gave him a good-natured scowl and then made a show of teasing the buttons open on her blouse. After John and Ray had encouraged her with wolf-whistles and cries of '*Strip! Strip! Strip!*' she eventually pulled the blouse away and tossed it across the room. The garment fluttered idly to the floor. Casually she passed the deck of cards to Ray and sat waiting for him to deal.

Her bra was crimson and lacy. Against her peaches and cream complexion the fabric looked rich and inviting. The bra was possibly a size too small because the swollen flesh of her breasts seemed to bulge over the cups with a sumptuous abundance. The shadow of a dark semi-circle sat near the edge of one cup, as though the bra wasn't quite concealing the upper edge of one areola.

And then they were playing again with Cassidy sitting at the table in her bra and Beth holding a pair of tens. All of them, Beth noticed, were pretending this was perfectly normal.

Of course, Beth told herself, it *was* perfectly normal.

She had seen Cassidy wearing only a bra on numerous previous occasions. When they had been helping one another get dressed for a girls' night out, and when they had been shopping for clothes, it was not unusual for them both to see one another wearing only bra and panties. Beth had even seen Cassidy naked in the changing rooms at the swimming baths. But there was something different about the atmosphere in the room this evening that made Cassidy's state of undress seem lurid, torrid and darkly exciting.

Beth resisted the urge to drain the alcopop John had brought for her. She was fearful the influence of alcohol would be calamitous in these circumstances. And she had only just composed her thoughts to focus on the game when she realised Cassidy was winning the second hand of the evening.

'Beth,' Cassidy exclaimed excitedly. 'I want Beth to take off her fleece.'

Beth shrugged as though the matter was of no importance. She tried not to blush as she slipped her arms from the sleeves. But removing the jacket felt like the start of something enormous. She allowed the fleece to fall to the floor and then took the deck of cards from Ray. Within moments she realised she had dealt another winning hand to Cassidy. The realisation made her stiffen with dread.

'I want to see Beth take her top off.'

'Why do you want to see me naked?'

Without waiting for a response, Beth pulled the T-shirt over her head. She was thankful that the bra she'd picked for the evening was one of the nicer ones from her collection. A white T-shirt bra with lacy scallops around the cups. The fabric shone crisply against her spray-tanned skin and it matched the thong beneath her jeans. She quietly hoped that no one else in the room would get to see that thong before the end of the evening. The thought made her cheeks burn crimson. The heat in her face intensified as she realised she was suffering the scrutiny of John, Ray and Cassidy. And her loins simmered at a heat that was driving her mad with need.

'Seriously, Cassidy,' she began. She spoke quickly, hoping none of them would hear the nervous excitement in her voice. 'Why do you want to see me naked? Have you turned into a predatory lesbian?'

'I've always wanted to see you naked.' Cassidy breathed the words in an exaggerated husky whisper. She smoothed a finger against the tip of her bra, as though teasing her own nipple. Feigning sexual elation, she sighed. 'You drive me horny with desire, Bethany.'

Beth flipped her the finger.

Ray laughed.

John shook his head and glanced at Ray. 'This is the life, isn't it?'

Ray grinned. 'Beer. Poker. Rock music. And two sexy women in bras, both sitting so close we could touch either of them.' They raised their beer bottles and tipped a salute to each other. 'This holiday is finally starting to improve.'

And then John dealt a winning hand to Ray.

Ray said he wanted Beth to take off her shoes.

Even before she had finished complaining about the injustice of being the one asked to undress after every hand, Beth found herself staring in amazement as Cassidy placed down a royal flush.

'This can't be happening,' Beth said in dismay.

'Jeans,' Cassidy told her.

Beth rolled her eyes. Her cheeks had turned a furious pink. She stood up and, without trying to make the gesture look like a seductive striptease, she unbuttoned her jeans and then smoothed the denim down her legs. She half-expected Ray and John to make encouraging sounds but, this time, they remained silent. In the background David Coverdale from Whitesnake was fading out with his repeated refrain of 'Is this Love'.

And, for the first time, she understood the game had now turned serious.

'What happens ...' John paused before finishing the question. His usual façade of cool and calm was momentarily flustered. He licked his lips and then glanced at Cassidy. 'What happens if Beth loses the next two hands?'

All three of them turned to stare at Beth.

She wanted to squirm in her seat. Their attention was a rare combination of intrusive but exciting. Her flesh prickled as though her skin was being teased by their collective gaze.

'If Beth loses the next two hands,' Cassidy began, 'then

she's going to be sat there naked. I suppose the real question is: what forfeit do we make her do if she loses the next *three* hands?'

Beth swallowed. Tilting her head defiantly, she said, 'Deal the cards and let's see what happens. I have to lose the next three hands before we start talking about my forfeits.'

Whitesnake began to play the opening bars to 'Here I Go Again On My Own'. Ray dealt the cards. Beth's heart thudded swiftly in her chest. She tried not to think about the arousal building inside her body. She silently prayed that her nipples would not grow hard for fear that the stiff tips would be noticed through her bra. Glancing down at her chest, noticing the embarrassing thrusts that now jutted at the front of her bra, she figured her prayers had been ignored.

Hoping no one noticed that her hands were shaking, she took a swig from her bottle of alcopop.

It seemed, despite the faults with the weather, the holiday had proved a constantly arousing experience. During the first night, after they had all piled their suit-cases into the appropriate bedrooms, John and Cassidy had mumbled a hurried excuse about needing to get some sleep. The creaking from their bed had been audible and Beth had fallen asleep to the rhythmic sounds of her friends making love. The following morning she had been woken by Cassidy crying out. At first she had thought her friend was in pain – a muscle spasm or stubbing her toe on the unfamiliar landscape of the bedroom furniture. It was only later that morning, when Cassidy blushed beneath the question, that Beth realised her friend had been shrieking through an early-morning orgasm.

And it wasn't just John and Cassidy who were enjoying the libido-enhancing benefits of the holiday. Beth had been pleased to think that she and Ray were making the bed in their own room creak long and loud into the night. She also thought they were behaving more intimately and more daringly than they had been in the months prior to the holiday. She smiled as she thought of the way they had been petting in the car earlier that day as they dashed to a nearby supermarket for supplies. Ray's fingers had slipped beneath her skirt. Her hand had cupped him through his jeans. And they had acted like a pair of horny teenagers hidden by the constant downpour of the rain. The memory made her smile. She squeezed the muscles of her inner thighs and savoured the echo of pleasure that mimicked the earlier afternoon's thrills.

'Full house,' Cassidy cried.

Her shrill voice shattered the fond memories of Beth's car-park frolics with Ray.

'I don't believe it,' Beth complained. She laid down three kings and a pair of tens. 'A full house. Why don't I have this sort of luck when we're playing for money?'

But she barely heard her own words. Blood was pounding through her temples with the force of a raging torrent. She had an idea what was going to happen next and she couldn't decide whether it would be perfect or purgatory.

'Lose the bra.' Cassidy spoke as she shuffled, without even glancing up in Beth's direction. 'Let's see those puppies set free.'

'Result,' John muttered.

Beth was mortified to hear Ray chuckle in agreement. Blushing crimson, and thrilling from the excitement of the moment, she reached behind her back to find the clasp of her bra.

It wouldn't open.

Her fingers tried to grasp the flimsy hooks and they fumbled awkwardly. She frowned, the difficulty of the task sapping the pleasure from the experience. She had wanted to appear cool about the forfeit, as though it meant nothing to her. But, as she realised everyone was watching her, she silently squirmed beneath the attention.

'Let John give you a hand with that,' Cassidy suggested. 'I can see he's dying to help.'

Beth stiffened. She could easily imagine John's strong fingers against her. She could picture his coarse manly knuckles rubbing softly against the sensitive skin of her back as he unfastened the clasp. The thought made her dizzy with unexpected need.

She had often told Cassidy that she was lucky to have a partner as attractive as John. But she had never considered him sexually desirable before. Now, with the vivid idea of his fingers unfastening her bra placed clearly in her mind's eye, it was impossible not to think about John's strong fingers touching other parts of her body. She could imagine him cupping her breasts. She had a mental picture of him teasing her nipples and then suckling against one. Then she could imagine his fingers moving down to her groin and touching –

'Go on,' Cassidy insisted. 'Let John unfasten that for you. I'm sure he won't mind.'

Beth glared at her. 'Ray can do it for me,' she said stiffly. She turned her back to her husband, presenting him with the clasp.

It was only when she had moved her position that she realised she was facing John. With her back to Ray it meant, as soon as the bra was opened, she would be thrusting her bare breasts towards Cassidy's husband.

He smiled at her.

His gaze was fixed on hers as he raised one eyebrow into a silent question.

Her nipples had been stiff before. Now they hardened to a point that was nearly painful. A rush of fluid heat seared her loins. She held her breath, knowing that she was in danger of sighing with desperate need.

'What's going to happen if Beth loses two more hands?'

Ray asked. The words trembled through his fingertips as he touched his wife's bare back. His knuckles pressed lightly against her spine as he released the clasp.

Beth quickly wrapped an arm across her chest to cover her modesty.

John flashed an approving scowl. 'Enlighten us, Cass,' he said easily. 'I'm interested to know and, since you seem to have made up all the rules for this evening ...'

'I suppose we're all adults here,' Cassidy said softly. She glanced first at Ray, then Beth and then John. 'If this game of strip poker went further than simple nudity ...'

Beth struggled to discreetly remove the bra while the men were distracted by Cassidy's seriousness. She was determined to play along with the game, but it was not in her nature to ostentatiously flaunt her bare boobs. Keeping one hand tight across her chest, she used her fingers to tug the unfastened straps from her shoulders.

'... if we ended up swapping partners for one night,' Cassidy continued, 'I think we're all mature enough to handle such a situation. Wouldn't you agree, Beth?'

Beth knew that Cassidy had waited for this moment to ask her the question. It meant that every eye was turned in her direction as she tried to wriggle discreetly out of the bra. She fixed her friend with a hot expression that barely scratched the surface of Cassidy's equitable smile. 'We're drinking alcopops, listening to rock music and playing strip poker,' Beth said testily. 'I don't think it's the dictionary definition of maturity.'

Ray made to pass her the cards but Beth simply glared at him. She had one arm draped tight across her chest and no intention of moving it so that she could deal the cards.

'You deal for me,' she told him. There was enough insistence in her voice so that no one dared to argue.

Ray passed the cards around the table.

And Beth wondered if he was now imagining what it would be like to fuck Cassidy. Her own thoughts were a jumble of daring ideas that involved herself and John. They were both naked. They were alone in a darkened room. She was submitting to his dark and intimate kisses. She was allowing him to explore her nudity while she touched him and tasted him and savoured the experience. And, as a background to those physical sensations, she could hear Ray and Cassidy gasping eagerly on a creaking bed as they fucked and fucked and –

'Fuck!' Cassidy snapped.

Beth glanced up, wondering if Cassidy had read her thoughts.

'This is a lousy hand,' muttered Cassidy.

'I think Beth's holding a decent pair,' John quipped.

Ray and Cassidy laughed too loudly. Beth blushed but she had to admit she was touched by the compliment. She wondered if John would tell her she had a decent pair if he had spent a furious half-hour sucking against her nipples and heightening her need for him through a bout of forbidden partner-swapping foreplay. The idea made her so wet she was sure pre-orgasmic tremors were bristling up and down the inner muscles of her sex.

Ray shifted position.

John wriggled, as though he was uncomfortable, and Beth instantly knew that both men had moved their postures because they were nursing uncomfortable erections. If she had been able to see through the wooden surface of the coffee table she knew that she would have seen the bulge thrusting at the front of her husband's jeans. More excitingly, she knew she would have been able to admire the thrust of John's arousal.

'The best I've got is a pair of threes,' John said. He kept casting glances towards Beth's breasts. It was obvious he was no longer interested in the card game.

'That beats me,' Cassidy said. 'The highest card I've got is a ten.' She threw the cards on to the table with disgust.

'I've got a king,' Ray admitted.

They all turned to stare at Beth. She awkwardly picked up her cards from the table, managing the task without allowing too much bare breast to be exposed. She was holding a pair of aces. Without needing to look at the community cards she knew she had won. Her heartbeat raced.

'Aces,' she said brightly.

Cassidy nodded. 'You won. You get to name the loser. And you get to decide what the loser has to remove.' She paused and said, 'Is this where you get your revenge on me? Are you going to make me take my bra off?'

Beth considered her response. Still keeping one arm across her chest, she reached for her drink and took a long thoughtful swig. After a moment she came to her decision.

Slowly, Beth stood up. She allowed her hands to fall to her hips so that she was openly displaying her bare boobs. Ray, she noticed, was gracing her with an approving smile. John, Beth was delighted to see, was staring at her breasts with obvious avaricious desire. She glanced at Cassidy and was pleased to see her best friend give a companionable wink. It was an enormous decision to make. But, because Cassidy had already pointed out that they were all mature adults, Beth felt sure this was the right thing to do.

'Since everyone has been wanting me to get naked this evening, I might as well give in to popular demand,' she said firmly. Not waiting for a response, smiling against the deafening pounding of blood that rushed through her temples, she hooked her thumbs into the waistband of her thong.

The air had been electric before. Now it was unbreathable.

Not allowing herself to think about her actions, convinced that this was exactly what she wanted, she pushed the thong down. She pushed it down past her knees, and squatted until it fell to her ankles. When she stood back up she was naked. Her exposed sex was on eye level with Cassidy, Ray and John. Beth imagined that the labia would be glistening wetly in the cottage's cosy light.

'Why on earth did you do that?' asked Cassidy.

'I got to pick who was the loser, didn't I? I figured I'd give you all the thrill of seeing what I've got before I take it upstairs.'

Cassidy's mouth worked soundlessly for a moment. 'You're going to bed. But I thought …'

Beth ignored her. She stared at John and said, 'I'm tired of losing at cards. I think I'm ready for bed now. Care to join me?'

And, as she allowed John to stand up, take her hand and then lead her from the room, she called over her shoulder to her husband and best friend. 'Goodnight, you two,' she said softly.

Aiming a wink somewhere between Cassidy and Ray, she added, 'Don't do anything I wouldn't do.'

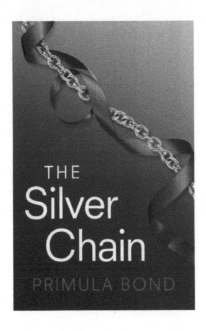

THE SILVER CHAIN – PRIMULA BOND

Good things come to those who wait…

After a chance meeting one evening, mysterious entrepreneur Gustav Levi and photographer Serena Folkes agree to a very special contract.

Gustav will launch Serena's photographic career at his gallery, but only if Serena agrees to become his companion.

To mark their agreement, Gustav gives Serena a bracelet and silver chain which binds them physically and symbolically. A sign that Serena is under Gustav's power.

As their passionate relationship intensifies, the silver chain pulls them closer together. But will Gustav's past tear them apart?

A passionate, unforgettable erotic romance for fans of *50 Shades of Grey* and Sylvia Day's *Crossfire Trilogy*.

GAME – JUSTINE ELYOT

The stakes are high, the game is on.

In this sequel to Justine Elyot's bestselling *On Demand*, Sophie discovers a whole new world of daring sexual exploits.

Sophie's sexual tastes have always been a bit on the wild side – something her boyfriend Lloyd has always loved about her.

But Sophie gives Lloyd every part of her body except her heart. To win all of her, Lloyd challenges Sophie to live out her secret fantasies.

As the game intensifies, she experiments with all kinds of kinks and fetishes in a bid to understand what she really wants. But Lloyd feature in her final decision? Or will the ultimate risk he takes drive her away from him?

Find out more at www.mischiefbooks.com

POWER PLAY – CHARLOTTE STEIN

Now she's the boss, everything that once seemed forbidden is possible…

Meet Eleanor Harding, a woman who loves to be in control and who puts Anastasia Steele in the shade.

When Eleanor is promoted, she loses two very important things: the heated relationship she had with her boss, and control over her own desires.

She finds herself suddenly craving something very different – and office junior, Ben, seems like just the sort of man to fulfil her needs. He's willing to show her all of the things she's been missing – namely, what it's like to be the one in charge.

Now all Eleanor has to do is decide…is Ben calling the kinky shots, or is she?

Find out more at www.mischiefbooks.com

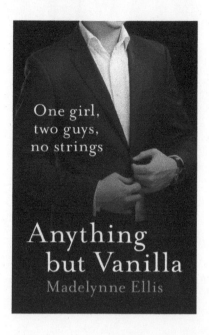

ANYTHING BUT VANILLA
MADELYNNE ELLIS

One girl, two guys, no strings.

Kara North is on the run. Fleeing from her controlling fiancé and a wedding she nev
wanted, she accepts the chance offer of refuge on Liddell Island, where she soon
catches the eye of the island's owner, erotic photographer Ric Liddell.

But pleasure comes in more than one flavour when Zachary Blackwater, the charmi
ice-cream vendor also takes an interest, and wants more than just a tumble in the su

When Kara learns that the two men have been unlikely lovers for years, she becom
obsessed with the idea of a threesome.

Soon Kara is wondering how she ever considered committing herself to just one ma

Find out more at www.mischiefbooks.com

www.ingramcontent.com/pod-product-compliance
Ingram Content Group UK Ltd.
Pitfield, Milton Keynes, MK11 3LW, UK
UKHW022246180325
456436UK00001B/26